DEADLY DOCTOR

JENNA ST. JAMES

Deadly Doctor

Jenna St. James

Published by Jenna St. James

❀ Created with Vellum

❧ 1 ❧

"Are you finding town life any easier?" I asked my cousin, Serena, as she unclamped Zoie's long hair from the curling iron.

"Not in the least." Serena gathered the sides of Zoie's hair and clipped them together in the back, leaving a few tendrils loose to frame Zoie's face. "I'm still not sleeping well."

Almost two months ago, my cousin, Serena, had married the love of her life, Detective Grant Wolfe. Since Serena and her best friend, Tamara, had lived together in a small cottage outside town, Serena felt it only fair she move out and live in Grant's house and give Tamara the cottage and small parcel of land. It only took Serena a week to realize she hated living in town.

"At first," Serena continued, "I tried to pretend everything was fine, but Grant knows me too well. I miss my little cottage and garden. The town noise keeps me up half the night, and I'm now relying on sleeping potions to help me sleep."

"I'm so sorry," I murmured as my boyfriend's teenaged daughter, Zoie, turned to give Serena a hug.

"You guys are too sweet," Serena said, patting Zoie's back. "So now Grant and I are looking for a place, but you know how impossible that can be on Enchanted Island. Most homes are passed down through generations here, and new homes are rarely ever built unless someone has serious money. Our realtor said she has nothing outside of town right now."

"Enchanted Island is a pretty big place," Zoie said. "I'm sure something will come available soon. I have faith."

I motioned for Zoie to twirl around so we could examine her from all sides. Even though Valentine's Day wasn't until tomorrow, the high school's big dance was tonight, and she looked killer in a red slinky dress with matching heels.

"You look amazing, Zoie," I said. "Brick won't know what hit him."

"That's the idea," Zoie said.

I smiled at her enthusiasm, but I knew she was still struggling with what had happened a few weeks back. Getting a call from Alex's old partner, Kara Hilder, telling us Zoie's mom had surfaced in another supernatural town after being gone nearly six years had been a blow to both Zoie and Alex. We'd all traveled to Mystic Cove to confront Camille, and the fallout had been heartbreaking. But at least now we didn't have to wait for the other shoe to drop. Camille would not attempt to contact Zoie again—per Zoie's wishes.

Zoie picked up her cell phone and gasped. "Brick should be here in ten minutes. Do I need anything else to finish this outfit?"

Serena nodded. "A necklace. Do you have one? If not, I can conjure up one for you real quick."

Zoie slapped her forehead. "I totally forgot I promised Ms. Twinkle I'd stop by and pick up a necklace she wanted to loan me to go with my dress."

Ms. Twinkle was a charming woodland fairy who lived next

door to Alex and Zoie, and who was currently seeing Doc Drago, the town's medical examiner. They both claimed the dating was casual, but I had high hopes it would turn into something more. I made it a point to wave to her every time I stopped by Alex's place and saw her outside.

"No problem," I said. "Serena and I will run next door and get it for you."

"Thanks." Zoie grabbed a tube of lipstick off her dresser. "Just a few more touches, and I'll be ready."

Serena and I headed downstairs, but when I saw Alex and Needles—my flying and talking porcupine bodyguard—staring out the window in the living room, I stopped and gave Alex a kiss.

"Serena and I need to run next door and get a necklace for Zoie. I guess Ms. Twinkle offered to let Zoie borrow one of hers."

Alex smiled. "That sounds like something Ms. Twinkle would do. She's such a nice woman." He leaned his forehead against mine. "You'd think these school dance nights would get easier, but they don't. I'm a nervous wreck."

"So am I," Needles said, his wings a dull gray. *"It's probably a good thing I never had little porcupines of my own."*

"And why is that?" Serena asked.

"Because this stress is too much for me to take! All of my quills would have fallen out long ago…and what kind of warrior would I be without my quills?"

Serena laughed, Alex groaned, and I shooed Needles away. My dad, Black Forest King, insisted I keep Needles with me at all times for protection. But honestly, I think Dad just wanted to let Needles out of the forest. Give the old warrior porcupine something to do in his later years…which equated to driving me crazy.

And I wasn't the only one. Ever since the explosion that blew up my Bronco with Needles inside, everyone who was there for the incident could now hear Needles talk.

I leaned up and kissed Alex again. "We'll be back with the necklace in just a second. Brick should be here any minute."

"We'll be prepared," Needles said. *"The young vampire-witch may seem on the up and up, but I always have my eyes on him."*

Alex gave me a "help me" look…which I promptly ignored.

Serena and I hurried out the front door, crossed through both yards, and climbed the steps to Ms. Twinkle's front porch.

I knocked lightly on the door, but no one answered.

"Guess she's not home," Serena said.

I knocked louder on the door, and was surprised when it creaked open. "I don't think it was latched." I pushed the door open and stuck my head inside. "Ms. Twinkle? Are you in here?"

There was no answer, but I could hear the TV down the hall in another room.

"What should we do?" Serena asked.

"Go inside. She told Zoie she would have a necklace for her. We'll just let her know we knocked, and the front door wasn't shut."

I pushed the door open all the way, and Serena and I stepped inside the dimly lit foyer.

"Oh, my goddess!" Serena exclaimed. "Is that blood?"

On instinct, I reached for my gun, only to realize I didn't have it with me. I wasn't in my game warden uniform…I was in plainclothes because it was a Saturday night, and I was helping Zoie get ready for a high school dance.

"Get your magic ready," I whispered.

Serena nodded.

I stepped farther inside the foyer, and I instinctively knew if that was Ms. Twinkle's blood, we wouldn't find her alive. The blood splatter was tremendous. I pointed down the hallway and could just make out a trail of blood droplets.

Whispering a spell, I quickly conjured up gloves and crime scene booties, then handed a pair of each to Serena before snapping on my own. "I don't want us to contaminate anything."

Serena quickly donned the gear. "Should we call for help?"

"Let's just wait and see what we find."

Serena nodded. "Okay. Could be we're worried for nothing."

I didn't think so.

"Ms. Twinkle?" I called out. "This is Shayla Loci. Are you okay?"

Serena threw up a light orb, giving us the ability to see farther down the hallway.

"Oh, crap!" I started to run, careful to leap over the blood in the corridor.

A pair of feet stuck out from the doorway on the right. Bending down, I turned the body over and winced. It was Ms. Twinkle, all right, and it looked like her throat had been slashed. A piece of paper, held in place by a knife, was pinned to her chest.

"Bring the light orb closer," I said to Serena. "I want to read the note."

Serena did as I requested, and we both gasped.

Written in red ink were the words: "Ten years later, and someone must pay. A life for a life, for love taken away. Tic-Toc, Doc."

2

Doc Drago looked like he'd aged ten years as he knelt down next to Alex and me…and the dead body of Mrs. Greta Twinkle, the woman he'd been casually dating for a few months now. Standing three feet from the body, Finn Faeton—a five-foot-nothing sprite with multi-colored spiked hair, body tattoos, and piercings in her nose, eyebrows, and ears—was combing the area looking for clues and bagging evidence she could later process.

It had taken a lot of convincing, but Alex and I finally persuaded Zoie and Brick to go to the Valentine's Day dance. Both had wanted to stay behind since they knew Ms. Twinkle. But staying home wouldn't change Ms. Twinkle's situation, so they finally piled into Brick's car and headed to the school dance.

Needles, not keen on dead bodies, volunteered to stay at Alex's house and keep watch from the porch to make sure the killer didn't return to the scene of the crime. Not that he knew what he was looking for…it was just a way for the porcupine to save face, so he didn't have to stay around the dead body. Serena had called Grant, then offered to go back to Alex's place and make coffee for the long night ahead.

"Body is just going into rigor," Doc said gruffly. "She probably hasn't been dead but maybe two or three hours."

"You okay?" I asked.

"No, I'm not okay." Doc stood and paced in front of the body. "Why? Why now? It's been ten years. Why would someone wait until now to bring up the past?" He ran his hands over his face. "And why take it out on Greta? She never did anything to anyone here on Enchanted Island. She's only been on the island for a year now."

Alex and I stood and guided Doc away from the body.

"I'm still new myself," Alex said. "Tell me what this is about."

Doc sighed and ran his hands over his face again. "Ten years ago tonight, the night before Valentine's Day, my wife, Marta, was driving home from her best friend's house when she had an aneurysm and died."

"I'm so sorry," Alex said.

Doc nodded. "Thank you. The worst part was, she hit an oncoming car and killed the driver of that car as well."

Alex's eyes met mine. "And who was driving the other vehicle?"

"Lena Craft. Sweet lady. She was married, but they never had children."

"I vaguely remember her," I said. "I think she volunteered down at the library when I was a kid. Dark hair and always wore dresses. That's what I remember."

"That was Lena," Doc said.

Alex shifted his stance. "Is it possible Lena Craft's husband is behind this?"

"I can't imagine," Doc said. "Bernard Craft is a bit…strange, but I don't see him murdering someone ten years after his wife's death. He still lives on the island, and I know he blames me, but he's never outright threatened me." Doc shook his head. "I can't see him suddenly doing something like this."

"Did Lena Craft have any brothers or sisters?" Alex asked.

"Her parents have both passed away since the accident ten years ago," Doc said. "She has a sister, Lorraine, but she's since moved off the island. Lorraine's daughter, Jessica, still lives here. But again, I can't see Jessica doing this. She was only a teenager when this all happened, if I remember right." Doc closed his eyes. "Besides, Lena's parents and sister seemed to understand it was a freak accident."

"We'll still want to question Jessica," I said.

"Anyone else angry at you about what happened that night?" Alex asked.

Doc sighed. "Marta's brother." Doc looked down at the floor and closed his eyes. "My brother-in-law, Seamus Oakleaf, blamed me for Marta's death. He moved to some secluded place outside town after Marta died ten years ago and has refused to speak to me since."

Alex frowned. "Why would your brother-in-law blame you?"

"He thought I should have known what was about to happen." Doc snorted. "Like being a medical examiner somehow gave me insight into the future." Doc wiped a tear from his eye. "Trust me, if I knew what was about to happen to Marta, I'd have given my life to save her."

None of us said anything for a moment…just let Doc compose himself. It was tough seeing the stalwart dragon shifter so emotional.

"What about Dr. Wandman?" I asked. "Don't you guys have…issues?"

Doc smiled. "We've been rivals for more years than I can count, but I can't see him doing this, Shayla."

"Dr. Wandman, the dentist?" Alex asked.

Doc nodded. "Yes. Howard and I have always been rivals. But, again, I don't see him taking another person's life."

Alex frowned. "Other than being a rival, why kill Greta Twinkle? I don't see the connection for a motive here."

Doc cleared his throat. "Before I came back from medical school many, *many* years ago, Howard and Marta used to date. When I moved back to the island to take the job as medical examiner, Marta and I started to see each other. That's another reason Howard hates me."

Alex nodded. "Now I see. Anyone else who might want to get back at you for any reason?"

Doc shook his head. "I honestly can't think of anyone else."

"So we have Bernard Craft—Lena's husband at the time of her death," Alex said, writing the names down on a tiny notebook. "Seamus Oakleaf—your former brother-in-law, and Dr. Howard Wandman?"

"That's about it," Doc agreed.

"Good place to start," I said.

Doc looked over at Greta's dead body. "I should tell her family what's happened."

"I have Deputy Sparks covering that," Alex said. "It might be too fresh coming from you."

Doc nodded. "Right. I hadn't thought of that. I'll start the autopsy tomorrow. I should know more by tomorrow afternoon."

"Over here!" Finn yelled, placing something in one of the evidence bags. "I got a hair that doesn't belong to the victim. Totally different color and texture. I'll run it for DNA."

"You can remove the knife and note now," Alex said. "I know normally Doc would do that since it's on the body, but I don't want to chance the paper getting torn or destroyed in the move."

Finn nodded, and we once again stood back from the body while she went to work.

"Tell me about Greta Twinkle, Doc," Alex said. "Why do you think she was targeted?"

"I started seeing Greta in the early fall. Everything was fine, things were going well with us, but with the holidays coming up, she wanted to back off and spend more time with her family. They were, after all, the reason she moved to the island." Doc shrugged. "After the holidays, we picked back up. We probably saw each other about once or twice a week. It wasn't serious, just casual. But nice." Doc smiled. "She was the first woman I'd dated since Marta's death all those years ago."

My cell phone rang, and I yanked it out of my jeans' pocket. "Hey, Mom. I can't talk right now."

"Is it true?" Mom demanded. "Is Greta Twinkle really dead?"

I sighed. "How did you know?"

"Mrs. Wolfinski down the street from Greta's house just called and said the police and medical examiner are at Greta's house. Is she dead?"

"I can't discuss it right now," I said. "You know there's an order to these things."

Mom sniffed. "She was a kind woman. Who would want to kill her? She's not even lived on the island that long." Mom paused. "Come over after you've finished there and we can talk then. You can spend the night. Make sure you invite Alex and Zoie over for Sunday morning breakfast."

I sighed. It was pointless to argue with Mom when she set her mind to something.

"Okay. See you in a few hours."

I disconnected and shoved my phone back inside my pocket.

"Lots of spectators outside," Detective Grant Wolfe said as he eased down the hallway, careful not to contaminate the scene.

Alex nodded. "Figured as much. Grant, starting tomorrow, why don't you run background checks on Howard Wandman, Bernard Craft, and Seamus Oakleaf."

"Got it," Grant said, scribbling the names down in his notebook.

Alex clasped a hand on Doc's shoulder. "We'll get to the bottom of this, Doc. I promise. Until then, I want to see if we have any eyewitnesses. Grant, you take across the street, and Shayla and I will hit up the houses on my side. We need to find someone who saw what happened here tonight."

❧ 3 ❧

Fifteen minutes later, dejected and cold, I blew on my hands while Alex answered his cell phone.

"Hey, Grant. Tell me you have something for me?" Alex paused, then smiled. "Shayla and I will be right there."

"He find someone?" I asked.

Alex nodded. "Two doors down. Kid was taking out the trash for his mom earlier tonight, and he thought he saw something."

We crossed over two yards, grabbed a coffee from Serena in Alex's front yard, then crossed the street and walked over to where Grant, a thirty-something woman, and a young boy of about ten stood in a yard three houses down.

"This young man is Lee Nightman," Grant said. "Why don't you tell Sheriff Stone and Agent Loci what you told me."

The boy's eyes lit up, and he nodded enthusiastically, his shaggy hair falling into his eyes. "Yeah, sure thing. I was taking out some trash for my mom. It's on the side of the house over there, so I have a pretty good view of Ms. Twinkle's house. She's real nice to me. Always giving me candy and stuff like that." He paused and kicked the ground. "I'm real sorry someone hurt her."

Alex laid his hand on the boy's shoulder. "Just tell us what you saw. It might help us find out who hurt Ms. Twinkle."

The boy nodded and blinked back tears. "Okay. Like I said, I've got a pretty good view of Ms. Twinkle's house from the side yard, and tonight, while taking out the trash, I saw Ms. Twinkle open her front door. At least, I thought it was Ms. Twinkle. I was gonna yell out hi to her, but then I noticed it wasn't Ms. Twinkle." The boy frowned. "The person was too big to be Ms. Twinkle."

"What do you mean, too big?" Alex asked.

The boys shrugged. "Dunno. Just that it didn't look like her. Ms. Twinkle is real thin and short. This person was tall and a lot bigger." He scrunched up his face. "But I think it was a woman. I mean, she was wearing a long dress, so it must be a woman, right? That's all I really noticed before she walked down the street and left."

"Did you get a look at this person's face?" Alex asked.

The boy shook his head. "Too far away. I just noticed how big the person was and that it couldn't be Ms. Twinkle."

I nodded. "Good. Did you see what kind of car this other person got into?"

Lee shook his head. "Nah. Mom hollered at me to hurry up and come inside because I needed to set the table for dinner. So I ran back inside. I didn't think anything more about it until mom and I heard the sirens, and then Detective Wolfe came by to ask us questions."

Lee's mom wrapped her arms around her son's thin shoulders and pulled him close to her. "I'm sorry about Ms. Twinkle. If there's anything else we can do to help, just let us know. She was a lovely witch."

"I hope you catch that bad woman soon," Lee said, lifting his small chin in the air. "She needs to pay for what she did."

"I agree," Alex said. "And we'll do our best."

The three of us waited until Lee and his mom went inside their house before speaking.

"Reliable?" Grant asked.

"Seems to be," Alex said. "So we're looking for a tall woman?"

"Or someone dressed as a woman," I said.

"What doesn't make sense," Alex said, "is the fact our suspects are all men. Yet, Finn found a long hair, which I assume belongs to a woman. And now we have a witness saying they saw a woman fleeing from the scene. So who did Doc forget to tell us about?"

"Hopefully," Grant said, "Finn can get a name from the hair. Make this case a lot simpler."

I nodded and took a sip of my coffee. "I say we start again in the morning. It's late, and it could be Finn gets a hit tomorrow on the hair and murder weapon."

"I agree," Alex said. "Grant, you and Serena go on home. We'll start again in the morning."

Grant closed his notebook and nodded. "Don't forget. Valentine's Day dinner at our house tomorrow night."

I snorted. "I still can't believe you guys are putting on this big shindig. I mean, it's your first Valentine's Day as a married couple, and instead of being all secluded and telling us to stay away, you two are putting on a huge dinner for everyone."

Grant looked at Alex and grinned. "Well, you know Serena. She loves nothing more than a reason to celebrate."

"Next time try celebrating alone," I suggested.

Grant laughed and sauntered across the street to gather up Serena and take her home. I could see the blue shimmer of

Needles' wings from the front porch. A sure sign he was tired and sad.

"I'm going to stay the night at Mom's. She wants you and Zoie to come over for Sunday breakfast."

Alex pulled me close and kissed my forehead. "We'll be there."

By the time I got Needles in my Bronco and pulled into Mom's driveway, I was emotionally and physically drained. Dragging myself from the vehicle, Needles and I headed inside to the safety of Mom's house. She'd lived in this house since she moved out of the castle years ago. She once told me living in the castle Dad had built for her when I was a baby was too painful, and she needed to distance herself from his pull. I got the feeling she still struggled with her decision to move away from Black Forest and the castle.

"There you are," Mom said from the sofa, setting her cup of steaming tea on the coffee table. "Would you like some tea? It's still hot in the kettle."

"No, thanks."

"I'm exhausted, Princess. I'm off to bed." Needles zipped out of the room and headed toward his favorite place to sleep at Mom's house—in a basket of blankets in Mom's library.

"Sit down," Mom said as she tucked her feet in underneath her, "and tell me everything."

4

"Happy Valentine's Day," Alex said as he handed Mom and me each a box of candy and then a vase of flowers.

"Oh, Alex," Mom blushed, gathering the flowers and candy in her arms. "It's been a long time since a man has given me gifts on Valentine's Day."

If I had to guess, I would say it had been forty years, but I didn't say that aloud. Instead, I gave Alex a kiss and buried my nose in the roses and inhaled. "Lovely. Thank you."

"I got candy and this pretty bracelet." Zoie stuck out her arm. "Isn't it beautiful? It's amethyst and black tourmaline. It's a protection bracelet."

I bent down and examined the bracelet. "Nice job, Alex. It will definitely do the trick."

"Yep," Needles said, his wings glowing green and yellow. *"That will definitely do the job. The gargoyle did good with this gift. I approve."*

"Thank you, Needles," Alex said dryly. "Your approval means everything to me."

"I got heart-shaped pancakes this morning," Mom said from the stove. "Alex, you pour some coffee and sit down at the table. Shayla and Zoie can get out the maple syrup and set the table."

Alex poured himself a cup coffee and sat down at the table. Needles, eager for a paw full of maple syrup, hovered near my shoulder.

"So how was the dance?" I asked Zoie. "Did you have fun?"

Zoie nodded as she used her magic to get down the plates and send them to the table. "I suppose. I'm still so sad about Ms. Twinkle. I can't stop thinking about her."

We sat down to breakfast and tried to keep the conversation light and away from Ms. Twinkle's murder. Needles didn't gorge on Mom's food like he normally does, so he wasn't passed out from a food coma when we gathered our things to leave.

"I think I'll ride with you today, Princess," Needles said.

Alex stared at me, but I just laughed. "Sounds good, Needles."

Needles thought it was his job to chaperone Alex and me during work hours, and no matter how many times I tried to convince him he had nothing to worry about during our working hours, Needles still insisted.

"Don't forget about Serena's dinner party tonight," I said to Mom.

Zoie clasped her hands together. "I'm so excited. Dad let me buy two dresses the other day. One for the dance at school last night, and the other for tonight's party."

I threw up my hands. "Why is it I'm the only person who thinks this is a crazy idea? Those two should be at some supernatural bed-and-breakfast on the mainland this weekend. Not cooking for twenty-some people."

"You know your cousin," Mom said, wiping down the counter. "She loves this kind of stuff."

Fifteen minutes later, Alex, Needles, and I exited Alex's Blazer and walked up the cracked sidewalk to Bernard Craft's house.

It was one of the older homes on the island, and Bernard had done nothing to restore or repair it. Located southwest of town, the houses were spread apart and surrounded by trees.

The three of us stopped short when we came upon a rather gruesome sight. Bernard Craft was sitting in a rocking chair on his front porch, and next to him, rocking in a similar chair, was a skeleton dressed in a burgundy dress and a dark-haired wig. She was reading a magazine and didn't bother to look up when we approached.

Needles dropped to my shoulder. *"Nope. Not going another inch. That is not normal."*

I had to agree with him, but we had a job to do.

"For once," Alex said, "I have to agree with the porcupine."

Before we could take another step forward, Bernard Craft leaned forward and spat over the porch railing. "Whaddya want?"

"That's attractive," I grumbled. "Mr. Craft, Sheriff Stone and I need to speak to you about the death of Greta Twinkle."

"Don't know her."

Even though Bernard had stopped rocking, the skeleton in the chair next to him had not. She was still reading her magazine and turning pages.

"Okay," I said, stepping up to the railing, "how about we talk about Doc Drago, his wife, Marta, and what happened to your wife, Lena, ten years ago last night."

Bernard leaped out of the rocking chair, his face flushed red. "How about we don't!"

"We can do this here," Alex said, "or we can do it downtown. Your choice, Mr. Craft."

For a few seconds, Bernard said nothing. The only sound was the creaking of the rocking chair as the skeleton moved back and forth, turning her pages in the magazine.

"Fine. But you stay right there. You ain't welcome on my porch."

I didn't want to go on his front porch or anywhere else near the animated skeleton made to look like his dead wife…so I was okay with that request.

"That's fine," Alex said. "Do you blame Doc Drago for the death of your wife?"

"Of course I do!" Bernard exclaimed, spittle flying from his mouth. "His wife's carelessness killed my wife!"

"What happened was an accident," I said.

"I lost my wife because *his* wife was driving her car when she died."

Alex shifted and widened his stance. "Last night was the ten-year anniversary of Lena's death?"

"That's right. So what?"

"I'll fly down the chimney and look around inside," Needles said. *"See what other kind of freaky things he has going on."*

Before Alex or I could stop him, Needles flew from my shoulder up to the chimney top.

"Are you aware there was a murder in town last night?" Alex asked. "A Ms. Greta Twinkle was murdered."

"Already told you," Bernard Craft snapped, "I don't know no Greta Twinkle."

"She'd been seeing Doc Drago," I said, "and when she was found, she was found with a note pinned to her chest. The note referred to the accident that happened ten years ago. Are you still going to deny knowing Greta Twinkle?"

Bernard narrowed his eyes. "I am."

I crossed my arms over my chest. "Where were you last night between four and seven?"

"I was here at my house," Bernard said.

"Can anyone vouch for you?" I asked.

Bernard pointed to the still moving rocking chair. "If Lena here could speak, she would tell you."

"Oh, good grief," Alex whispered.

Needles dropped from the roof and settled back down on my shoulder. *"This guy has seriously lost his marbles. You should see the inside. There are a bunch more skeletons all wearing the same wig, but wearing different colored dresses, and they're all doing different things. One skeleton is watering the plants, another is vacuuming, and there's even one baking in the kitchen. Positively gruesome and unnatural."*

"Let's talk about what happened ten years ago," Alex said. "What can you tell me about the night Lena died?"

Bernard stared past my shoulder. "Sheriff Hawkins came to my door and told me there'd been an accident. When we arrived at the accident site, Doc was already there. I was told the accident happened around nine-thirty."

"That's pretty late," I said. "Where was your wife coming from?"

"Her mother's. After dinner, Lena went to visit her mother on the northwest side of the island and give her the box of candy she bought for her for Valentine's Day. After that, she was going to run to the grocery store down the street from her mom's. She told me she needed to get some ingredients to prepare my favorite meal the next night." His face turned red, and he gripped the arms of the rocking chair so tightly, his knuckles turned white. "Only she never got to make me that dinner, because Marta Drago killed my wife!"

"Thank you for your time, Mr. Craft," Alex said. "If we have any more questions, we know where to reach you."

Bernard Craft didn't say a word as we turned and headed back toward the blazer.

"That was beyond surreal." I buckled my seatbelt. "I can't believe he's animated all those skeletons and has dressed them in Lena's old clothing."

"I can't decide if it's sick," Alex said as he backed down the driveway, "or some sweet, yet macabre, dedication to his wife."

"It's sick," Needles said from the back.

"Does it take a lot of magic to do something like that?" Alex asked.

I shrugged. "I'm not sure. To do it every day, I want to say yes."

"So he'd be considered a powerful witch?" Alex asked.

"I don't think so. I mean, Mom and GiGi have never said anything about him having powerful magical abilities." I frowned. "Something about what he said bothered me."

"What's that?"

"He said his wife went to the grocery store to get some last-minute items after leaving her mom's. The only grocery store on the northwest side of the island is Fireson's Grocery. A dragon shifter family has owned it for generations. Their hours have been the same since I was a kid. They close every night by eight."

"Okay."

"If Lena went to the grocery store and left by eight to go home—which is just a fifteen minute drive from the northwest side to the southwest side where she lived—where was Lena for that hour and a half before the accident?"

Alex turned his head and looked at me. "That's a great question. Do me a favor and text Grant and tell him to pull the file on

Marta's and Lena's accident. I want to go over it carefully. We've just started questioning people, and already we have red flags. Also, see if he can track down Jessica's last name—Lena's niece—and have him go pay her a visit."

"On it." I pulled out my phone and sent Grant a quick text. "Who're we questioning next?"

"I could use a salt stick back here," Needles whined. *"All that creepiness has left my salt intake too low. I'm getting faint and dizzy."*

I rolled my eyes and dug out a bag of pretzels from my backpack. "Here you go." I threw a large pretzel stick to the back. "We wouldn't want you to faint on us."

"Speak for yourself," Alex said good-naturedly. "Let's go see what the brother-in-law, Seamus Oakleaf, has to say."

5

Finding Seamus Oakleaf's house was a little harder than we thought it would be. To say Seamus was now living off the grid deep in the woods would be an understatement. At one point, I thought we were going to have to ditch the Blazer and walk the rest of the way to Seamus' cabin. Luckily, the Blazer enjoyed off-road driving.

The haphazard cabin looked like it had been slapped together with dead logs and sorrow. There was no other way to describe it. The outline of the exposed brick chimney was almost completely covered with thick, thorny vines that reached the top of the roof. Even the porch was riddled with holes.

"I feel like this entire investigation should be happening around Halloween and not Valentine's Day." Needles dropped to my shoulder. *"Everything is so bleak and spooky."*

Alex knocked on the door, and a few seconds later, a man dressed in brown pants and a white t-shirt pushed open the screen door.

"Yes?"

"Mr. Oakleaf?" I asked.

"That's me. What can I do for ya?"

"I'm Agent Loci, and this is Sheriff Stone. We need to talk to you about something that happened in town last night."

"Don't see how I can help. I came out here to get away from everyone after my sister died. I don't go into town much anymore."

"Instead," Needles said, his wings glowing black and red, *"you just sit out here and plot murders?"*

"Do you know Greta Twinkle?" I asked.

Seamus' brows furrowed. "I don't think so. I don't get out much anymore, like I said. Just my weekly trip into town for groceries and to run errands."

"Can you tell us where you were last night between four and seven?" Alex asked.

"Why?" Seamus asked.

"Because Greta Twinkle was murdered last night," Alex said, "and there was a note pinned to her chest referencing the fatal accident that happened to your sister ten years ago."

For a few seconds, Seamus said nothing. Then he shrugged and stepped outside onto the porch, letting the screen door close behind him. "I don't know anything about it. Like I said, I don't know a Greta Twinkle."

"Let's go back to where you were yesterday," I said. "Where were you between four and seven?"

Seamus sighed. "Let's see. I ran into town around three-thirty to put fresh flowers on Marta's grave for the anniversary of her death. After that, I came straight home."

"What time would you say you arrived home?" I asked.

"I guess around five. Stayed at the gravesite for quite a while to talk with Marta." His eyes filled with tears. "I miss her a lot. Even after all these years."

"Do you blame Dr. Drago for your sister's death?" Alex asked.

"Yes! Most definitely."

"Why?" I asked. "Marta died from an aneurysm. How could he have known?"

"He's a doctor!" Seamus exclaimed. "He should've seen her symptoms. He should have known this was going to happen!"

"I don't think that's how it works," I soothed.

Seamus snorted. "What do you know? The morning of Marta's death, I spoke with her on the phone. She seemed confused about everything. When I asked her if she was okay, she said she had a headache. I told her to call Doc and ask him to come home and give her something. But she said no, he was working. It was always like that with them. She didn't want to disturb him at work. It was always about him. Never about her! Never about Marta."

"She must not have said anything to Doc about the headache and confusion when he got home," I said, "because she went out later to visit her friend."

Seamus shook his head and looked away.

Alex shifted beside me. "So you blame Dr. Drago for the death of your sister?"

"Yes!" Seamus hissed, still staring out into the woods. "You have no idea what all Drago took from me the night of the accident."

I frowned. "What do you mean?"

Seamus glanced back at me. "Why are you asking me all these questions about that night? Why dredge it all back up?"

"Because what happened ten years ago to Marta Drago and Lena Craft has come full circle," I said. "Whoever killed Greta Twinkle last night made sure we knew it had to do with what happened the night Marta and Lena died."

"I can't help you any more than I already have," Seamus said. "I moved out here to get away from the gossip…not to become a part of it."

Alex and I thanked him, and then walked back to the Blazer.

"What do you think?" Alex asked as we bumped down the rutted road.

"He was in town during the timeline we've established for Greta's death," I said. "And it's obvious he hates Doc and blames him for his sister's death. We definitely have to keep him on the suspect list."

"At least he wasn't as nuts as that Bernard Craft fellow," Needles said.

6

Dr. Howard Wandman lived on two acres in a sprawling ranch-style brick house on the west side of the island. When we pulled into the driveway, both garage doors were up, and Wandman was inside tinkering around.

"What do we know about him?" Alex asked as we exited the vehicle.

"I think I remember Mom telling me once he'd been married like three or four times."

"He should give up trying," Needles said.

"I've already heard," Howard Wandman said as we approached the garage. "I'm in complete shock. I can't imagine who would want to hurt Greta."

"So you knew her?" I asked.

Howard nodded. "Yes. Greta and I dated for a couple months over the summer." He shook his head and scowled. "Then out of nowhere, she tells me she wants to see other people."

"Do you know who that other person was?" I asked.

Howard scowled. "Drago!"

"You're referring to Dr. Drago?" I mused.

"I am." Howard looked away and blew out a sigh. "Can you tell me how Greta died?"

"We still need the medical examiner to give us the official cause," Alex said, "but it looks like her throat was slashed, and she was found with a note pinned to her chest with a knife."

Howard dropped his head into his hands. "That's horrible. What did the note say?"

I glanced at Alex and he nodded, giving me the go-ahead. "Ten years later, and someone must pay. A life for a life, for a love taken away. Tic-Toc, Doc."

Howard's head jerked up, and his hands fell away. "I didn't kill her! I cared for Greta!"

Alex nodded. "Okay, then. Tell us where you were between four and seven yesterday."

"I played golf with some buddies, and we finished around three. I had a late lunch at the clubhouse. I then ran a couple errands—dry cleaning and grocery store—and then I came home."

"Do you have a copy of the receipts?" I asked.

Howard frowned. "Why?"

"Establishes a timeline for when you were there," I said.

Sighing, Howard reached into his back pocket and pulled out his wallet. "Here."

I took the receipt and saw the timestamp of four-ten. "So you picked up your dry cleaning a little after four, and then you went to the grocery store. You probably returned home around a little after five?"

Howard shrugged. "I guess."

"Can I see the receipt for the groceries?" I asked.

Howard scowled. "I didn't keep it."

"But you kept your dry-cleaning receipt?" Alex mused.

"I can take off dry cleaning on my taxes. I can't take of groceries."

"Oh, he's a clever one," Needles mused from my shoulder.

"Let's talk a little about Marta Drago," I said.

Howard crossed his arms over his chest. "Why?"

"You dated Marta *years* ago before she married Doc, is that right?" I asked.

"You know it is."

"How did you two meet?" I asked.

"When I came back to Enchanted Island from the supernatural dentistry college I attended after high school, eight years had passed. Marta was younger than me, so I didn't really know her. But upon my return to the island, I went into a business where she was working as a receptionist. I asked her out, and we dated for four years. I was about to propose to her over Christmas, when Doc returned to the island after being gone twelve years." Howard scowled. "And in true Drago form, he comes back being the king—strutting around as the new medical examiner."

"Blasphemy!" Needles hissed, grabbing two quills out of his back as his wings glowed red. *"Black Forest King is the only king on this island."*

Howard looked at Needles and frowned. "Why does he look all crazy? Almost like he's rabid."

I sucked in a breath. Howard had done it now.

"Rabid? I'll show him rabid!" Needles zipped over to within an inch of Howard's face, quills pressed against his now-huge eyes. *"I've been meaning to have me a tongue sandwich today, Witch. Yours will taste delicious roasted over an open fire."*

"Simmer down," Alex murmured.

"Needles," I said, "I'm sure he didn't mean to upset you."

Howard Wandman lifted his hands in surrender. "I'm sorry.

I'm sorry. Tell your—tell this Needles I didn't mean anything by the rabid comment."

"He can understand you," Alex said dryly.

"Fine," Howard said, "then I take it back. I take everything back."

Needles continued to glare at Howard for another heartbeat before dropping the quills and flying back over to my shoulder.

"Okay," Alex said. "Let's go back to when you and Marta were dating, and you were about to propose to her over Christmas. Then Doc Drago comes back to the island and what? You and Marta broke up?"

Rage flashed in Howard's eyes. "Four days before Christmas. Four days! I was about to propose to the woman I loved, when Marta sits me down and gives me this sob story about how she and Drago had fallen in love over the span of a day. A day! She's sitting there going on and on about love at first sight!"

"What did you do?" I asked.

"I'm sure you know the story," Howard said between clenched teeth. "I confronted Drago. It got heated, and Doc ended up with about ten stitches, and I ended up with this scar." He pointed to the scar above his eyebrow. "Doc also ended up with my future wife."

Alex nodded. "You seem to have a lot of hard feelings toward Dr. Drago."

"Wouldn't you? The man has done nothing but made my life miserable. I mean, seriously. I've heard the rumors about you two. What if some man came along and snatched Shayla out from under you, Sheriff? Wouldn't you be mad? That's exactly what he did with Marta." He scoffed and shoved his hands in his pockets. "And then, years later, Doc does it *again* to the new woman I was dating. Just stepped in and started dating Greta.

Trust me, it makes you angry." His eyes went wide. "But not angry enough to kill!"

"Thanks for your time," Alex said.

As we turned and walked away, Howard's cell phone rang. I could hear him talking to the person on the phone about being shocked to hear Greta had been murdered.

"What do you think?" Alex asked as he turned over the Blazer's engine.

"He acknowledges he was in town during the time of Greta's murder," I said. "Plus, he has a lot of hatred for Doc, and I'm sure still some lingering rage at Greta for dumping him to date Doc."

Alex nodded. "Yeah, he definitely stays on our suspect list. And, for the record, you better not get your head turned by some other man."

I laughed, pulled him close, and gave him a quick kiss.

"Seriously?" Needles whined. *"I'm sitting right here. And I just ate. Don't make me lose my salt stick."*

7

The Enchanted Island Sheriff's Department, the medical examiner's office, and the forensic labs were all located in one building—sheriff's office on the ground floor, and labs in the basement. Both departments were run with a firm hand by octogenarian twin witch sisters, Opal and Pearl.

"I don't want to go down there with the dead body," Needles said, his wings glowing dark blue.

"I'll unlock the sheriff's office so he can stay in there." Alex quickly unlocked the door and pushed it open so Needles could enter. Once Needles was inside, Alex locked the door.

"Did I hear right that Opal and Pearl are both out of the office for a few days?" I asked as Alex and I descended the stairs.

"Valentine's Day weekend getaway," Alex said. "This time she, Pearl, and the new husbands are at a supernatural resort in Hawaii bungee jumping off cliffs."

"No way!" I exclaimed as we bypassed the empty front desk and headed down the hallway to Doc's lab.

Alex chuckled. "Yep. They're due back late tomorrow night."

Alex knocked once on Doc's door before pushing it open. Doc and Finn were huddled together near a computer screen.

"I was about to call you two," Finn said. "I just gave Doc my findings."

"What did you find?" Alex asked.

Finn glanced at Doc. "Fingerprints on the knife and a hit on the hair."

"You're kidding," I said. "Someone was dumb enough to leave their fingerprints behind on the murder weapon?"

"Sure did," Finn said as she continued to stare at Doc. "And I got a hit."

"Who," I demanded.

"Christine Mossman," Doc said softly.

"That seems anticlimactic," I said.

"I agree," Alex said. "We have three solid suspects, and now we find out it's a woman no one ever mentioned."

"Who is Christine to you?" I asked Doc.

Doc closed his eyes. "She was Marta's best friend. She was the person Marta had gone to visit the night she died."

That statement hung heavily in the air.

Alex nodded. "Makes sense. The boy, Lee, mentioned he saw a woman exiting Greta Twinkle's house."

"It doesn't make sense," I argued. "I mean, Christine's motive to kill Greta Twinkle would be what? She found out Doc had been seeing Greta and believed he couldn't see anyone but Marta for the rest of his life? Like somehow Doc was cheating on Marta after all these years?"

Doc cleared his throat. "Possibly. But there was also a time after Marta had died when Christine thought we might get together after I finished grieving. I had to tell her gently that that wouldn't happen."

I nodded slowly. "So maybe Christine snapped? It was the

ten-year anniversary of her best friend's death, and she decided to take out her anger and heartache on someone Doc had been seeing? I guess it makes more sense now."

"Nothing about this makes sense," Doc said. "But I do have my report ready. It's as we thought. Cause of death was the slit throat. The knife to the chest was done postmortem."

"Tox report shows no traces of drugs or alcohol in Greta's system," Finn said.

"Time of death was between four and six," Doc added. "So we were on the mark with that."

"When's the last time you spoke to Christine?" Alex asked Doc.

"Maybe two months ago?" Doc said. "Yes, that sounds about right. She sent me a box of chocolates and nuts for Yule."

"Did you speak to her personally?" Alex asked. "Or did she just drop off the box?"

"I spoke with her. She seemed to be getting along okay." Doc frowned. "Although, now that I think about it, she did ask me how I was holding up, knowing this was the ten-year anniversary of Marta's death."

"Did she mention Greta?" Alex asked.

All the color drained from Doc's face. "Yes. She said she heard I was dating Greta Twinkle and wanted to know how it was going. I didn't want to divulge anything about us taking a break until after the holidays, so I just said things were good." Doc scrubbed his hands over his face. "Did I get Greta killed with that statement?"

"Don't go there," I said. "It's a rabbit hole you can't get out of."

Alex pulled out his cell phone. "Grant? Can you do me a favor and go pick up Christine Mossman and bring her in for questioning?" Alex nodded. "Sounds good. See you within the hour."

8

By the time Grant got back to the station with Christine Mossman, it was a little after three. I'd heated burritos in the work room microwave since Alex and I hadn't taken a timeout for lunch. Needles had eaten his weight in pretzels and was snoring away on the copy machine.

"Looks like the backgrounds on our other three suspects are finished," Alex said from Grant's desk.

"Good. I'm still not convinced it's going to be this easy. I mean, why would Christine leave her prints on the murder weapon? The young witness, Lee, didn't make it sound like the killer fled from the house. It's like they just strolled out. So why not take the time to wipe off the prints?"

"Looks like you'll get the chance to ask her."

Christine Mossman was a twittering ball of energy when she walked through the door with Grant. Dressed in red polyester pants and a red and white top, she was either dressed the part as a cold-blooded killer…or she was ready for Valentine's Day. I could tell she'd done a glamour spell on her face, but even that couldn't hide the effects of aging one hundred percent.

"Sheriff! I have a roast in the oven," Christine said as she batted her fake eyelashes at Alex. "I have a special someone coming over tonight, and my roast better not end up dry."

"We wouldn't want that." Alex motioned for Grant to take her into the interview room.

"She's cooking for a special someone?" I mused once Christine and Grant were down the hall. "Does she not realize she's a suspect?"

"Let's go find out."

We walked down the hallway and stopped in front of the interview room. Alex motioned to Grant.

"What's up?" Grant asked as he closed the door behind him.

"Why don't you go on home?" Alex suggested. "Deputy Sparks comes on the clock in about an hour, so if we detain Christine, he'll be here overnight with her. No sense you waiting around here as well."

"You're sure?" Grant asked. "You don't want to go over the backgrounds I gathered this morning?"

Alex shook his head. "Let's worry about that tomorrow. By the time we get done with Christine, it'll be pretty late. We'll barely make it for the Valentine's Day dinner Serena is putting on." Alex smiled. "And we definitely don't want to keep Serena waiting."

Grant grinned, and something passed between the two men, but I wasn't sure what it was. "Then we'll see you both in a few hours."

"You ready?" Alex asked once Grant had left the hallway.

Nodding, I opened the door and stepped inside the interview room. Christine looked up from the table and smiled.

"Oh, thank the goddess. I have to go soon. I have dinner in the oven."

"Grant didn't suggest you turn off the stove?" I asked as I sat down in one of the chairs opposite her.

"Of course, but I couldn't do that, dear. It would ruin my meal." She patted her bad dye job and smiled. "Wouldn't want my new suitor to think I can't cook."

"Ms. Mossman," I said, "are you aware of what happened to Greta Twinkle last night?"

"Oh, my yes. I heard this morning. Such a terrible thing. I can't believe it." She shook her head. "Used to be the island didn't have so much danger." She looked pointedly at Alex. "As the new sheriff, you should really do something about all this crime."

I bit my lip to keep from laughing.

Alex sat down in the chair next to me. "I'll keep that in mind, Ms. Mossman."

"How well did you know Greta Twinkle?" I asked.

Christine frowned. "How well did I know her? Well, I guess I knew her enough to wave at her when I saw her on the street or at the supermarket. Why?"

"Were you aware Doc Drago and Greta had recently dated?" I asked.

"Doc Drago? Yes, I think I remember hearing something about that. What's all this about?"

"Last night, when Greta's body was discovered, there was a note pinned to her chest. It referenced the deaths that had occurred ten years prior." I watched her closely. "The deaths of Marta Drago and Lena Craft."

Christine gasped and sat back in her chair. "No! Marta and Lena? But it's been years. Why would someone bring that up after all this time?"

Alex leaned forward across the table. "Exactly what we're trying to figure out."

Christine sat up straighter in her chair. "Wait. Are you saying you think *I* had something to do with all this?"

"We're just trying to get some answers," Alex said.

"That's code talk for you think I'm guilty!" Christine exclaimed. "I watch those cop shows on the television, young man. I know how you guys bring in someone and beat them down until they confess, even if they're not guilty." She lifted her chin in the air. "Well, you won't break me. I'll never confess because I didn't do anything wrong!"

Alex nodded. "Fair enough. Where were you yesterday between four and seven?"

"Yesterday?" Christine frowned. "Let's see, I was at Witchy Wands & Cuts until after three, getting a new color for my date tonight." She again fluffed her overly made up hair. "After that, I went to I Scream, You Scream for a treat. Their special this month is Hot Bloody Valentine—vanilla ice cream with red hots. There were at least five people who can verify that. Then I ran to Iris' flower shop to get fresh flowers. The shop was packed, of course, so I know someone there had to remember seeing me. Plus, Iris will have a record of my being at her shop buying the flowers." She pursed her lips. "Then after that I went to the grocery store real quick to get some strawberries and chocolate. After that, I came home and dipped strawberries."

"What time did you get home?" Alex asked.

Christine shrugged. "Probably around five-thirty. I dipped strawberries and had a quick bite to eat before heading over to my neighbor's house around six. Every Saturday night, we have what is called Saturday Night Sipping. Basically, we sit on the front porch, drink, and wave to people passing by. I was there until around nine."

I glanced over at Alex. It was a pretty solid alibi.

"Do you lock your doors faithfully?" Alex asked.

Christine's brows furrowed. "My doors?"

Alex nodded. "Yes. Do you lock them every time you leave the house? For instance, are they locked right now?"

"No. When the detective came to get me, I just closed the door. Why?"

Alex slid a picture of the bloody murder weapon across the table. "Do you recognize this knife, Christine?"

Christine's eyes widened. "That's mine! I can tell by the gouge in the handle. Happened about five years ago after—well, doesn't matter. I noticed the knife was missing a couple days ago, but I didn't think anything about it."

"Let's talk a little more about Greta Twinkle," Alex said.

"I didn't know her. I mean, I knew she moved to the island about a year ago to be closer to her daughter and grandkids, but that's all I really knew. We didn't hang out."

Alex folded his hands on the table. "We found your knife, with your fingerprints on the handle, and a hair matching yours at the scene of the crime. Can you explain that?"

"That's a lie!" Christine shouted. "You're trying to harass me to confess to something I didn't do!"

"It's not a lie," Alex said calmly.

Christine suddenly burst into tears, her mascara sliding down her face. "I don't understand any of this. I promise you, I didn't kill Greta Twinkle. Why would I?"

I slid a box of tissues closer to her. "Maybe you were jealous because she was dating Doc Drago?"

Christine huffed. "Oh, please. Why would I be jealous of that?"

I shrugged. "Maybe because you and Marta were best friends, and then after she died, you thought you could step in and take her place? And then when that didn't happen, on the night of her ten-year death anniversary, you killed the person who was now stepping into Marta's shoes?"

Christine's face turned red. "That's ridiculous! I've moved on. And I definitely wouldn't kill someone over a man. Even for someone as wonderful as Dr. Drago."

"That's not what the evidence says," Alex said.

Christine swiped at her tears, then blew her nose. "I demand an attorney. I'm not saying another word without an attorney."

"And you have that right." Alex stood. "Christine Mossman, you're being detained at the Enchanted Island Sheriff's Department for the next twenty-four hours, until an attorney can be arranged. Shayla will get you a phone so you can call your attorney."

Christine jumped up from the table. "I have to spend the night here? This is insane! I didn't do anything! What about my dinner in the oven?"

I stood and pushed my chair back. "Come on, Christine. You can use the phone in the front office. After you phone your lawyer, why don't you call your neighbor friend and have her run over and shut off your oven for you?"

"Wait? Are you saying I have to sleep in the jail cell?" She staggered and dropped back onto her chair. "Will I be with other prisoners? What if I get shanked and die in prison?"

I couldn't help the small laugh that trickled out.

Alex cleared his throat and stood as well. "There's only you here for right now, Ms. Mossman. Deputy Sparks is on duty tonight, so he will be in and out checking on you as he patrols the island."

"This is a nightmare! Why would someone do this to me? Who hates me enough to set me up like this?"

I met Alex's eyes over the top of Christine's head. I had to admit, there seemed to be way too much evidence pointing to Christine, when we had three perfectly good suspects already.

"I guess I can kiss a third date with my new beau goodbye," Christine grumbled. "He won't want to keep seeing a jailbird."

I ushered her out into the hallway and sat her down at Opal's desk. "Phone's right there." I turned to give her some privacy, then remembered what I wanted to ask her. "Christine, you were about to tell us how you got the gouge in the knife's handle we found at the scene of the crime."

"I don't want to tell you now. It will make me look even worse."

"How so?"

Christine sighed. "One night, about five years ago, right before we divorced, Howard and I got into a horrible fight. I picked up the knife and threw it across the room. It hit the wall, then bounced off a plate, and it chipped the wooden handle."

My mouth dropped. "Wait. Did you say Howard? Howard who?"

"Howard Wandman." She cocked her head and frowned. "You didn't know I was married to him for about two years?"

"I didn't. But I'm glad you told me."

9

"I can't believe we didn't know," Alex said as he turned onto Grant and Serena's street. "It's a good thing you asked her about the chip in the handle."

"This puts Howard even higher on my suspect list," I said. "Not only would he be hurting Doc by killing Greta, but he can also set up his ex-wife in the process."

"I agree, but we can't just throw out the facts we have in front of us right now. We need to question Christine further."

"You do realize you established reasonable doubt with the locked doors question, right?"

Alex grinned. "Yes."

"That's supposed to be her lawyer's job."

"I needed to know for my own sake," Alex said. "I think it points to reasonable doubt as well. If she doesn't lock her doors, anyone could have gotten inside to take the knife and a lock of her hair."

"And by anyone," I said, "I lean toward Howard Wandman."

"It's possible."

"Plus, our witness, Lee, said the person he saw fleeing Ms. Twinkle's house was tall and big. Christine is bigger than Greta, but I wouldn't exactly describe her as tall and big."

"I picked up on that as well," Alex said. "But, again, we follow the evidence. And right now, the evidence points to Christine. That doesn't mean we have to stop looking…it just means we have to hold her."

"I know."

I shook my head as Alex, Needles, and I got out of the Blazer. "It's like Serena invited the whole town to dinner tonight."

"A slight exaggeration, Princess," Needles snickered.

"Not by much." I looked down at my game warden uniform and groaned. "Not exactly the killer Valentine's Day outfit I was hoping you'd see me in tonight."

Alex wrapped his arm around my shoulder as we headed toward the front door. "You could wear a sack, and I'd still think you were hot as hell."

Needles made kissing noises as he flew ahead of us, his wings glowing red and pink.

I was about to knock on Serena's door when it flew open and Serena grabbed my wrist and dragged me inside. "It's about time! Hurry up." She thrust a champagne glass at me. "Drink this and go to my room and change."

"Change? I don't have anything to change into."

Serena rolled her eyes. "We have a house full of witches here tonight. Trust me, by the time we bibbidi-bobbidi-boo you, you're gonna look smashing."

"That's my cue to run!" Needles zipped out of the room, his pink wings fluttering nonstop.

"Grant is passing out the appetizers, and dinner is almost

ready. Alex, the men are in the kitchen, and there's beer in the refrigerator."

Serena gave me a shove up the stairs, and I quickly scrambled up them while taking a drink of the champagne. I pushed open Serena's bedroom door and groaned. Mom and GiGi were pacing back and forth, but stopped when Serena shut the door behind us.

"We've got five minutes," Serena said, yanking the flute from my grasp. "Let's work some magic here."

"I don't need—"

My words were cut off as my uniform disappeared and a red, lacy push-up bra with matching underwear appeared. Seconds later, my body was clad in a knee-length, red wrap-around dress with a startlingly low neckline.

I heard Mom whisper another spell, and my hair went from a messy top knot to long flowing locks down my back. GiGi performed a glamour spell for new makeup, and in less than three minutes, I had to admit, I looked amazing.

"Wow," I whispered as they turned me toward the mirror. "This all looks stunning."

"*You* look stunning," Mom said as she blinked back tears. "I'm not gonna cry."

I stole back the champagne glass Serena had taken from me. "Good. Now, let's go get something to eat. It's been a long day, and I'm starving."

When I walked downstairs, I noticed Alex had changed into dress pants and a royal blue button-down shirt. He'd been talking to Brick and Grant, but when he saw me, his mouth dropped.

"I brought a change of clothes for Dad," Zoie said as she gave me a hug. "The girls told me what they planned to do to get you ready, so I ran home real quick and got something for Dad."

"You did good, Zoie."

"You look gorgeous." Alex kissed me lightly on the lips and handed me another flute of champagne.

"At this rate, I'll be drunk before dinner." I snatched a chocolate-dipped strawberry off a passing tray the former sheriff, Walt Hawkins, was holding. "But I guess it could be worse."

I waved to Finn across the room, who was talking with Tamara, Zac, Jordan, and Baby Jayden. Shaking my head at the number of family and friends gathered together to celebrate a night of love, I took another sip of my drink.

"How did it go with Christine?" Doc asked as he sidled up next to me.

"Strange," I said. "Did you know she was once married to Howard Wandman?"

"Yes. They didn't last long."

"The more I think about this case," I said, "the more I'm convinced there's more to the story."

Aunt Starla thrust a tray of heart-shaped rolls filled with tomato and cheese at me. "Bread might help soak up some of that champagne."

I thanked her and popped one of the tiny treats in my mouth. "Where's Byron Seely? Did he not come tonight?"

Aunt Starla shook her head. "Poor guy came down with an awful cold. GiGi and I went out today to bring him soup."

GiGi had been seeing the selkie shifter, Byron, for a few months. We were all a little surprised the romance was still going on, but GiGi seemed happy with the relationship.

"I think you're right," Doc said. "I mean, I've known Christine for years. She's a tad bit shallow and self-centered, but she has a good heart. She's also a smart lady. I can't see her leaving fingerprints on the murder weapon."

"Can I have everyone's attention?" Serena called out. "Dinner is ready. And just so you know, Tamara and I brought home a lot of the Valentine's Day desserts that didn't completely sell out. So leave room."

Everyone laughed as we headed toward the two tables Serena and Grant shoved together. It was a tight squeeze to get everyone —including a highchair—around the table, but we did it. It wasn't long before I put the murder aside and focused on the food and fellowship around me.

I'd just taken the last bite of chocolate meringue pie and finished it off with the last of my champagne when Alex stood and turned to me.

"I know you said it seemed like Serena had invited the whole island out tonight," he said, "but the truth is, I asked her to put this together as a surprise."

I frowned and looked over at Serena…who was dabbing at her eyes with a napkin. And it wasn't just her. Pretty much all the women—including Zoie—looked about to cry. Even the men looked emotional.

"Okay," I said slowly, scanning the room for Needles. He was my anchor. If he looked upset, I knew there was something wrong.

Needles was perched on the hutch, his wings glowing blue, pink, and gray. I'd never seen a porcupine cry before…but I was sure he was about to explode. My stomach lurched, and I thought I was going to lose the pie I'd just eaten. Something wasn't right.

Alex reached down and helped me to stand. "I know how much family means to you, so I wanted them here when I did this."

"Oh, my goddess!" I exclaimed as reality set it.

Alex reached inside his pocket and withdrew a black velvet box. "Shayla, from the moment I met you working on our first case together, I knew you were special. You challenged me. You made me laugh. You made me want to pull out my hair." He reached out and grabbed my hand. "And even though you came with some baggage in the form of a talking and flying porcupine, I knew I wanted to get to know you better." He lifted my hand and kissed my knuckles. "The way you've taken Zoie under your wing so she could hone her witch powers, and then giving her a female role model she could be proud of—I knew there was no way I could ever let you go."

"*We* could ever let you go," Zoie piped up.

I laughed and looked over at Zoie, who was crying but smiling.

"*We* could ever let you go," Alex corrected. "Before you get too worried, I've spoken to Black Forest King and received his permission, along with your mom's permission."

I gave another watery laugh as tears blurred my vision.

"Shayla Loci, will you do me the honor of becoming my wife? Of becoming more than just my partner in the workplace, but my partner for life?"

"Yes!" I threw my arms around Alex and hugged him.

He eased me back, cupped my face in his hands, kissed me, then held out the closed velvet box. "I wanted to get you a unique ring that fit who you were, but I didn't know how to go about it. So a couple weeks ago, when we came back from Mystic Cove, I flew out to Black Forest to speak to your dad. Your mom met me there. I asked their permission to marry you, and then after their blessing, I told them I wanted to get you a special ring that embodied who you were. Your mom gave me this box."

I looked at Mom, who was wiping her own tears. "It's time you hear this, Shayla."

Alex opened the lid to the box. "Your mom never told you this, but when you were born, Black Forest King not only commissioned the castle to be built for you both, but he also gave your mom a ring. A ring she kept hidden and only wore when she was alone. This is the ring."

"What?" I gasped.

"It's true," Mom said. "It was too painful to wear, so I kept it hidden all these years. Now your father, Alex, and I would like you to have it."

I took the box from Alex and examined the ring inside. Rose gold, with a leafy vine entwined on either side of the band and coming together at the top to hold in place a moss green stone.

"It represents the forest," Mom said, "just as you, Shayla, represent the forest and animals within."

I slid the ring onto my finger, and this time, I didn't hold back the tears. Alex had given me the perfect ring.

"This calls for more champagne," Grant called out, "and a toast to the newly engaged couple!"

Drinks were poured, toasts were made, tears were shed, hugs were exchanged…and the night was perfect.

"I had the link to Black Forest King open the whole time Alex proposed," Needles said from my shoulder. *"I was able to tell him how the gargoyle was blundering it all."*

I laughed. "Thanks, Needles."

"My pleasure, Princess." He sprang in the air and hovered near my shoulder, his wings glittering red and pink. *"I am happy for you, Shayla Loci. I just hope this doesn't mean our working together will come to an end now that you will start a new life."*

I reached up and ran my hand over Needles' body as Alex and Zoie sidled up next to me. "Never. You and I are a team, Needles. Always."

"Hear that, Gargoyle? You'll never get rid of me now!"

"There always has to be that one crazy in-law," Alex said. "Guess now we know it'll be Needles."

"Was there ever a doubt?" Zoie joked.

10

"I assume you want to go see your dad?" Alex asked once everyone started to leave the dinner party.

"Do you mind?" I asked.

Alex brushed his lips against mine. "Not at all. I'll fly you out there, stay a while, then fly back here and get my vehicle before heading home."

"Sounds good. Let me say goodbye to Serena."

I found Serena in the kitchen with Mom and Zoie. They were laughing and chatting away as they used magic to wash and dry the dishes.

"You leaving?" Mom asked, standing up from the table.

"Alex and I are going to go see Dad real quick."

Zoie stood and lifted my hand, studying the ring. "I can't get over how beautiful this ring is."

"It's the perfect ring," I agreed.

She threw her arms around me and squeezed. "I'm so happy you and Dad are getting married."

I closed my eyes and hugged her back. "Me too."

Once Needles settled down inside the sweater I borrowed from Serena, Alex shifted and lifted us in the air. I'd flown to Black Forest a dozen times with Alex over the year, but this time was special. This time I was going to Black Forest so I could tell Dad I was about to get married.

I'd waited forty years to find the perfect gargoyle…for me.

We were starting our descent when the fireflies flew up to meet us.

"We just heard the news, Princess!"

"When will you be married?"

"Where will you be married?"

"This is a night for celebration!"

"Black Forest King is excited!"

On and on the lighting bugs chattered as we drifted between the pines, maples, and oak trees until Alex landed in front of the most magnificent tree in all of Black Forest.

My dad.

His tree roots were at least four feet tall off the ground and extended out about twenty feet from the base of the tree. He was nearly one hundred twenty feet around, with branches averaging thirty to forty feet. He was the largest tree in the forest…and nothing could shake him.

Dad was a genius loci, which meant he was literally the heart and soul of the forest.

Alex set me on the ground, and I closed my eyes and just breathed in the power around me. Everything about Black Forest was peaceful and grounding.

Just like Dad.

Needles flew out of my sweater and took off for Dad's treetop. That was his favorite place to perch while in Black Forest.

"I hear you have news for me, Daughter of my Heart," Dad said. *"Come closer and tell me about you and Alex Stone."*

Laughing, I ran and jumped up on his roots, then jogged down until I stood at his base. Flinging my arms around Dad's trunk, I held on tightly.

"I love the ring, Dad."

"I hoped you would. I commissioned it for your mother years ago in hopes she would one day pass it on to you." He chuckled. *"When the time was right. And I see the time is finally right."*

I dropped down and settled my back against Dad's trunk. Alex sauntered over and sat down cross-legged next to me.

"So tell me everything," Dad said. *"I want to hear it all."*

And so I did. I told him about Serena, Mom, and GiGi giving me a quick makeover. Of the wonderful food. And of the even more wonderful surprise Alex had given me.

"I assume young Zoie is happy as well?" Dad mused.

"Very much so," Alex said.

"I am happy for you both. You are exactly the type of supernatural I hoped for Shayla, Alex Stone. You and your daughter. It makes my heart happy knowing you will soon join to be a family."

A family.

I blinked back tears and reached for Alex's hand.

"I'm not ready to talk about *when* we're getting married," I said, "but I'd like to talk about *where* I'll be married. I want the wedding to be here in Black Forest. I want you to see me get married, Dad."

"Nothing would make me happier, Shayla."

"Would you be okay with just immediate family and close friends like Tamara and Finn coming? Plus, there's Kara Hilder and Zane who would probably want to be here. And Alex's parents from Seattle. But I promise there won't be more than twenty-five or thirty people in Black Forest. I know it's a lot to ask, and you've never opened the forest up to anyone besides

Mom and me, and now Alex, GiGi, and Zoie. But if you'd be willing, I'd love to have those closest to me attend."

"I see no problem with Black Forest accommodating up to thirty supernaturals."

I grinned and squeezed Alex's hand. "Good. Then it's settled, I think? Alex, are you okay with having the wedding here?"

Alex leaned over and kissed me lightly on the lips. "I'd love to have the wedding here."

"The townspeople may feel cheated," Dad said.

I shrugged. "Alex and I can have a reception in town the following week or when we come back from our honeymoon. We'll make sure we do something. After all, we both have jobs that deal with the public and the citizens of Enchanted Island. We wouldn't want to upset anyone."

"I think that's a good compromise," Alex said.

"Then it is settled. You will have your wedding here in Black Forest, and I could not be happier. Now, tell me about this murder Needles mentioned to me."

Thirty minutes later, Alex shifted and flew back to town to get his car and go home. We'd agreed to meet at the bakery at eight.

"I better get home, Dad. I'm emotionally and physically exhausted."

Needles threaded his way down Dad's branches, then settled on my shoulder.

"The fireflies will guide you back to the castle," Dad said.

Needles groaned. *"They'll talk the whole time, Black Forest King."*

Dad chuckled. *"I have no doubt they will. Be safe tomorrow, Daughter of my Heart."*

II

"We've already heard," Gertrude Anise said when Alex and I stepped inside the bakery the next morning. "When's the big day?"

I laughed. "I just got engaged last night, Mrs. Anise. Give me time to get used to that before you ask for a wedding date."

"Don't wait too long," Mrs. Anise grinned. "Someone may snatch him away from you. I may be nearing a hundred, but if I were a few years younger, I'd give you a run for your money, dear."

I laughed even harder. "I'm sure you would, Mrs. Anise."

"She can have him," Needles said as he zipped to the display case.

Alex sighed. "Why do I get the feeling Needles is going to be living with us even *after* we're married?"

I grinned and stepped up to the counter. "Because he will be."

"The usual?" Serena asked. "Two cinnamon rolls and two black coffees?"

"Sounds good," Alex and I said simultaneously.

"Why don't you give us a couple more cinnamon rolls," Alex said. "Our first stop is the station to go over suspects. I'm sure Grant could use the extra boost as well."

"You got it."

"Don't forget my salt stick covered in caramel sauce," Needles said, his wings glowing green and yellow.

Serena smiled. "Never. One caramel covered pretzel stick coming up."

As Serena got our order around, Alex's phone rang. He excused himself and took the call.

"Good morning, Shayla," Daisy Woods said as she sidled up next to me. "I heard the good news about you and Alex. Congratulations."

"Thanks."

I liked Daisy, a woodland fairy who worked for Mayor Stone. She was young, sweet, and knew just about everything going on in town.

"I can't believe Christine Mossman killed Greta Twinkle," Daisy said. "I'd have never guessed that."

"It was a surprise to us as well," I said.

"Poor Doc," Daisy continued. "First Marta dies, and then Marta's best friend kills his current girlfriend." She shook her head, her blond ringlets bouncing. "Just unimaginable."

"Doc's taking it pretty hard," I said.

"I can only imagine." She shuddered. "I guess I can just be glad nothing else crazy happened to Doc Saturday night."

I frowned. "What do you mean?"

"Well, I was out walking my dog Saturday around four o'clock, and I saw Bernard Craft sitting in his car, just staring at Doc's house."

I blinked in confusion. "Wait. Are you telling me that

Bernard Craft was in town in front of Doc's house on Saturday, around four o'clock?"

"Yes, why?"

"Because Craft told us he was at home," Needles said excitedly, his wings glowing green and purple. *"We got us a little liar."*

"No reason," I said, keeping my voice steady. "I just wanted to make sure I heard you correctly. Did you notice what time he left Doc's house?"

Daisy shook her head, her curls again bouncing. "Sorry, no. I didn't think anything else about it." She frowned. "Wait, I guess if I think about it, his car wasn't in front of Doc's house when I walked by again. I had to be home by four-thirty to feed Muffin and my other animals, so I could accurately say by four-thirty he was gone from in front of Doc's house."

"Smack dab in the middle of the timeline for Greta's murder," Needles said.

"Thanks, Daisy. You've been a tremendous help."

"Any time." She grabbed her fancy double mocha off the counter and bounced out the door.

"That was Christine's lawyer, Merlin Sage, from the mainland," Alex said as he sidled up next to me. "Sage says he should be on Enchanted Island by ten-thirty and at the station by eleven."

"Merlin Sage?" I mused. "Now *that's* a name." I grinned. "Oh, by the way, I just got *huge* news. One of our suspects has been lying to us. I'll tell you more when we get to the station so Grant can hear."

Alex raised an eyebrow. "Now I'm intrigued."

We pushed our way to the door, nodding at well-wishers and smiling at the good-natured ribbing from the excited citizens.

"Whew!" Needles said, landing on my shoulder. *"It's like these people have never seen two people engaged before."*

"They're just excited," I said, opening the door so Needles could fly inside.

"Hand me my salt stick, Princess. I'm about to starve back here."

I rolled my eyes, hopped up in the front seat, then turned and handed Needles his treat. By the time we arrived at the station, he'd eaten nearly a fourth of the tall, gooey pretzel.

"I need a nap," Needles whined as he nestled against my neck. *"All that sugar and salt makes me sleepy."*

"I'll get Needles a place," I said as we walked inside the station, "and then join you and Grant."

Alex nodded. "It's weird not having Opal here to harass me the minute I walk through the door."

Walking to the break room, I grabbed a tea towel, folded it into a tiny square, then carried it out to the bench seat under the front window where the sun was beating in. Needles dropped onto the towel, sighed, wrapped his wings around his body, and within seconds, I could hear his soft snores.

"He out?" Grant asked.

I nodded. "Yep. Doesn't take long when Serena doses him with salt and sugar."

"We should have her do that hourly," Alex said.

Grant laughed and unstacked the folders on his desk. "I don't have much in the way of background. No red flags on Howard Wandman, Bernard Craft, or Seamus Oakleaf. No arrests, no major debt. These three are fairly squeaky clean. I was able to pull a hospital stay for Bernard Craft about six months after his wife died in the car accident ten years ago. He went to a supernatural psychiatric hospital for three months on the mainland."

"No surprise there," I said, thinking of the animated skeletons. "Unfortunately, it didn't seem to help."

"That bad?" Grant asked.

I shuddered. "You have no idea. He has *skeletons* that are animated and dressed like Lena."

"You're kidding?" Grant mused.

"Not at all," I said.

"Glad you guys took that one," Grant said.

"So let's get to suspects," Alex said. "We know the murder weapon found at the scene of the crime where Greta Twinkle lived belonged to Christine Mossman. The murder weapon also had Christine's prints on them. We also know Christine was best friends with Marta Drago and even tried to date Dr. Drago after the grieving period. Doc said no, rejecting Christine. Then ten years later, Doc dates our victim, Greta Twinkle. We are going on the theory that Christine snapped on the ten-year anniversary of her best friend's death, killed Greta, then fled the scene, leaving behind evidence that proves she is guilty."

"Way too neat," I said.

"I might have to agree," Grant said. "Normally, I'd be excited how it all came together, but there are just too many unanswered questions for it to be this neatly wrapped up."

"So let's look at our next suspect," Alex said. "Howard Wandman. He and Doc have had this friction for years. We know at the time of Greta Twinkle's murder, Howard was in town running errands and golfing. In his younger years, he dated and was even going to ask Marta Drago to marry him. And, we now know that Christine—our main suspect—was once married to Howard for a couple years. If Howard Wandman is our killer, he would be successful in getting back at Doc and setting up his ex-wife to take the fall."

"He's definitely my prime contender," I said.

"Okay," Alex said, "then next, let's look at Bernard Craft. We know he was institutionalized after the death of his wife, Lena Craft. The accidental death was caused by Marta Drago. Bernard must blame someone, and since he can't blame Marta, he now blames Doc. We've seen how he holds onto the past."

"Yeah," Grant said, "dressing up a skeleton as your dead wife is definitely a red flag for me."

Alex nodded. "I would agree. The next question we have to ask is why would he set up Christine Mossman to take the fall?"

"That's where I'm having trouble," I said. "Other than the fact that Christine was Marta's best friend, I don't really see the benefit. It would be different if Doc and Christine had dated, but they never did. So why set up Christine?"

Alex nodded. "Plus, he wasn't in town at the time of the murder."

"That's where my big news comes in," I said. "Get this… Daisy Woods tells me this morning at the bakery that she remembers seeing Bernard Craft in his car, sitting outside Doc's house Saturday around four."

Alex and Grant were silent.

"Are you serious?" Alex demanded.

Grant chuckled. "I love it when we catch suspects lying."

I nodded. "Yeah, this definitely makes Bernard look guilty. But, again, what's the motive?"

"You and I are going to go pay Bernard Craft another visit this morning," Alex said, "but before we do that, let's finish up with our last suspect. Seamus Oakleaf, Marta's brother."

I nodded. "Well, we know Seamus definitely blames Doc for his sister's death. There's a lot of anger still when he talks about Doc and how he should have known Marta wasn't well. I'm fairly certain if we ask him, Seamus would know that Christine Mossman was Marta's best friend."

"But why set up Christine?" Grant asked. "What would Seamus have to gain?"

Alex folded his hands and rested them on the desk. "Maybe he knew at one point Christine tried to hit on Doc. You take the culmination of the ten-year anniversary and his anger at the situation, and maybe he thought Christine was the best fall guy or fall girl."

I shrugged. "Possibly, but I definitely think Howard Wandman and Bernard Craft have more to gain by killing Greta and setting Christine up."

"Speaking of Christine Mossman," Alex said, "how is she doing?"

Grant smiled. "Deputy Sparks told me this morning she raised a little Cain throughout the night, but nothing he couldn't handle. I stopped in to see her about thirty minutes ago, and she was still spitting mad."

I snorted. "She mad about the arrest or mad she'll have to find a new boyfriend?"

"I think it's more about the boyfriend," Grant said. "She asked me three or four times if I knew how hard it was to find a good, eligible man on Enchanted Island."

"There's one other crazy thing that's been bothering me," I said. "And that's the story that Bernard Craft told us about Lena and where she was the night the accident happened."

Alex nodded. "That's right. I forgot you told me about the grocery store."

"What am I missing, Shayla?" Grant asked.

"Bernard told us Lena went to visit her mom on the northwest side of the island, and then she was going to the grocery store. I know for a fact the grocery store she went to closes at eight o'clock. It always has. But the accident didn't happen until around nine-thirty. So where was Lena during that hour and a half?"

"I pulled the file." Grant opened the folder and shuffled through some papers and photos. "Here's the report."

I grabbed a couple of the photos and flipped through them as Alex read the report. A few minutes later, he lifted his head.

"Sheriff Hawkins states Bernard told him Lena had been visiting her mother and then stopped by the grocery store before coming home. That's everything about Lena in Walt's report."

Grant frowned. "Walt was probably more focused on the accident and how it happened."

"Maybe Walt can shed some light on this for us," Alex said. "Grant, can you get a hold of him and see if he can come in this afternoon and talk with us?"

Grant nodded. "I can do that."

Alex stood. "Good. I think it's time we take another pass at our three suspects. Christine's lawyer should be here in a couple hours. We should be back before then."

12

Three patients were sitting in the plush chairs of Howard Wandman's dental office when Alex and I walked inside. Needles had elected to stay in the vehicle and finish off his caramel pretzel.

"We need to speak to Dr. Wandman, please," Alex said as we ambled up to the counter.

The young receptionist blushed as she stood. "I'm sorry, Sheriff. The doctor is with a patient right now. Can you come back later?"

"I'm afraid not," Alex said. "It's important."

"Um, okay. Let me see…" She trailed off and looked over her shoulder. "Um, can you hold on a second?"

Alex nodded. "Thank you."

She scampered across the room to the back offices and returned in less than a minute. She cleared her throat and smoothed down her scrubs. "Dr. Wandman said you can go on back. He's waiting for you in his office. It's the second room on the left."

Howard Wandman was sitting behind his desk, his hands steepled over his chest. He tried to appear at ease…but I could see the strain around his eyes and mouth.

"What can I do for you?" Howard said. "I have a patient in the chair next door, so I'd appreciate it if we can make this fast, please."

"Sounds good," Alex said. "You were once married to Christine Mossman, is that right?"

Howard frowned. "Yes. For a couple years. Why is that relevant?"

Alex glanced at me, then back at Howard. "I take it you're not aware we currently have Ms. Mossman in our custody?"

Howard Wandman jerked to a sitting position. "What? In your custody, for what?"

"Her fingerprints were found on the murder weapon that killed Greta Twinkle," Alex said.

"That's ridiculous!" Howard exclaimed. "Why would…" His voice trailed off. "Really? I'm surprised. Or maybe not. I mean, we weren't married long, but she never stopped talking about Marta and Doc even long after Marta had died."

I crossed my arms over my chest. "How long did you say you two were married?"

"Let's see, maybe a year or two? That sounds about right. It's easy to lose track when you've had as many wives as I've had."

"How many times have you been married?" Alex asked.

"Three. First wife was Carrie Oakmont, second wife was Christine Mossman, and my third wife was Tish Biteman." He got a wistful look in his eyes. "She was a scrapper. Vampire."

"Thank you for your time," I said.

We walked out into the front office and out the door.

"We know Christine doesn't lock her house like she should," I said as I buckled my seatbelt, "so it would be nothing for him to get inside, grab a knife and lock of hair, and stage the murder scene."

"Definitely possible."

"Plus, did you notice how fast he was to throw her under the bus?"

Alex nodded. "Yep. Went from he couldn't believe it straight to he could see her doing it."

We drove in silence to Bernard Craft's house…the only sound was Needles chewing away on his salt stick. My cell phone dinged, and I read the text.

"Grant says he got a hold of Walt. He and a friend of his are out in the ocean fishing. Walt wants to know if he can come in tomorrow morning to talk about Marta's accident."

"Tell Grant that's fine," Alex said.

I quickly texted Grant with Alex's answer, then shoved my phone in my pants' pocket as I got out of the Blazer and followed Alex up Bernard Craft's driveway.

When Bernard opened the door and saw us, he scowled. "What? I answered all your questions yesterday."

"Actually," I said, "you may have answered them, but you didn't answer them truthfully. So we thought we'd come back and give you another chance."

"What're you talking about?" Bernard grumbled.

"Do you mind if we come in?" Alex asked. "This might take more than a few minutes."

Bernard sighed and opened the screen door. "Fine."

We stepped inside, and I immediately wanted to flee.

"I'm outta here," Needles hissed. *"I didn't sign up for this level of crazy."*

"I thought you were a big-time warrior?" I whispered.

"Yeah. And in the battles I won…the enemy stayed down. They didn't stand back up and do house chores."

Lena Red Dress was sitting on the sofa knitting a sweater, while Lena Blue Dress was bustling around dusting and cleaning. Seeing the bones of Lena Red Dress move effortlessly as she wound the yarn around the large needles was one of the creepiest things I'd ever seen in my lifetime.

And that was saying a lot.

"Mr. Craft," Alex said once we were seated—well, Craft sat next to Lena Red Dress on the sofa. I sat in a club chair with Needles ready to bolt off my shoulder, and Alex stood next to me. "It has come to our attention that you were not truthful when you told us you weren't in town at all Saturday. In fact, we have eyewitnesses that place you in front of Doc Drago's house around four that evening. Care to explain the discrepancy?"

Craft opened his mouth to answer, but before he could speak, Lena Flower Dress walked into the living room carrying a tray filled with cookies and a pot of tea with three cups. The skeleton set the tray down, then turned and left the room.

No way was I eating or drinking anything off that tray.

"Don't. Touch. Anything," Needles said.

Alex chuckled softly.

"Well, maybe you can have a cookie, Gargoyle."

Bernard leaned forward, snatched a cookie off the tray, ate it, then poured the tea.

"None for us, thank you," Alex said. "We just came from Enchanted Bakery & Brew."

"Your loss," Bernard said. "Lena makes the best cookies."

"Yeah. Cuckoo cookies filled with nuts, I bet," Needles muttered.

"That's quite an animation spell you're able to perform," I said. "How many do you have going at once?"

I couldn't bring myself to ask how many skeletons he had animated at once, but I figured he'd understand my question.

Bernard stopped chewing. "I have five versions of my wife." He reached over and patted Lena Red Dress. "It wasn't until the love of my life was snatched from me that I realized how hard she worked. It takes five Lenas to make up for the one I lost."

Lena Red Dress and Lena Blue Dress kept working, neither of them reacting to what Craft had said.

"If I have nightmares, Princess, I'm sending you the bill for the therapist," Needles said.

"I believe you were about to tell us why you lied," Alex said. "What exactly were you doing in town Saturday in front of Doc's house?"

"I was working up the nerve to go to Doc's door," Bernard said. "I was going to confront him on the ten-year anniversary of my wife's death and remind him of the pain he's caused me ever since his wife took my Lena away from me."

"And how were you going to remind him?" Alex asked.

Bernard looked away, and his jaw tightened. "I don't know. I hadn't gotten that far."

"Oh, he's definitely lying," Needles said. *"I'm surprised he didn't have one of these crazy skeletons just go inside and whack the good doctor."*

I looked up at Alex. Could it be that simple? Alex gave me a little nod, and I knew he'd picked up on the same thing I had.

"What time did you leave Doc's house?" I asked.

"Maybe around four-thirty," Bernard said.

"And where did you go after that?" I asked.

"Back home."

"Doubtful. I bet Mr. Crazypants here animated one of his skeletons, and the two of them went on a crime run over to Greta's place."

"Mr. Craft," I said, "do you know a Christine Mossman?"

"No, I don't think so. Why?"

"You didn't know Christine was Marta Drago's best friend?" I asked.

Craft shook his head. "Can't say I did."

"Really?" I mused. "I find it hard to believe you wouldn't know Marta Drago had been coming home from her best friend's house the night she had her accident. And I find it even harder to believe you don't know Christine Mossman."

Bernard Craft stared at me…but didn't say a word.

Alex sighed. "I think that's all the questions we have right now. If there's anything else you haven't told us, or we find out you've lied to us, the next time we question you, it will be in an official capacity down at the sheriff's station. Do you understand?"

"Yes," Bernard hissed between gritted teeth.

Lena Blue Dress set her dust rag on the shelf and walked us to the door. I could hear the pop and crack of her bones with each step she took.

"That was *so* creepy," I said as I opened my passenger door for Needles.

"Did you hear the way the skeleton rattled? That's not right." Needles picked up the last of his pretzel with his paw and started to chew. *"Nope. Not right at all. Gonna need therapy."*

The minute Alex got inside the Blazer, I rounded on him.

"Did you see that? I mean, this guy is nuts. I can totally see him dressing in one of his wife's dresses, breaking into Christine's house, and gathering the knife and hair. I can also see him going to Greta Twinkle's house, killing her, and leaving the note. All dressed as his late wife."

"Yeah, I caught on to that as well," Alex said. "Or maybe he animated one of his Lenas to do the killing?"

"We just may *think* we're looking for a woman."

"If Bernard is the killer," Needles said, *"will the Lena skeletons have to do life in prison as well?"*

Alex laughed. "Eat the rest of your pretzel and leave us in peace, Porcupine."

13

As Alex drove to Seamus Oakleaf's place, I tried to take my mind off the macabre scene at the Craft house. Instead, I thought about my upcoming wedding, the kind of dress I'd like, and who all would be there in Black Forest watching Alex and me get married.

"You coming in?" Alex asked.

I blinked and realized we were already at Seamus Oakleaf's cabin. "Sorry. I was thinking about the wedding."

"I'm gonna stay here in the vehicle. With the way this morning's investigation is going, I wouldn't put it past this guy to have some weird paranormal freak show going on inside his house."

Alex knocked on Seamus' front door, and a few seconds later, Marta's brother opened the door and stepped outside onto the porch.

"What now? Did you find another dead body you're trying to pin on me?"

"We just need to ask a quick question," Alex said. "Do you know Christine Mossman?"

"Of course I know Christine. She was my sister's best friend. Just as devastated as I was when Marta died. Poor girl took it hard." He shook his head. "Christine was like the sister Marta never had. Those two did everything together."

I nodded. "That's pretty much what Christine said about Marta. Are you aware Christine has been arrested for murdering Greta Twinkle?"

Seamus snorted. "I can assure you Christine Mossman didn't kill no one. She wouldn't have it in her."

"Her fingerprints and a hair belonging to her were found at the crime scene," I said.

Seamus said nothing for a few seconds...and then he shrugged. "I mean, I don't see why she'd kill this Greta woman. If she was going to kill anyone Saturday night, I would assume she'd kill Doc." Seamus scowled. "I know I would have if I was a murdering kind of man. He's the one to blame for everything I've lost."

I thanked him, and Alex and I headed back to the Blazer.

"He and his sister must have been *really* close," I said. "He always mentions what all Doc stole from him that night."

"I've noticed as well."

"Hey, it's Monday night." I hopped inside the vehicle, smiling at Needles snoring loudly in the backseat. "Is Zoie coming out to the castle and cooking dinner for us?"

Monday nights were my favorite because that's when Zoie normally came out after school and fixed Alex and me a proper, well-balanced meal. The girl could cook and bake almost as well as Serena.

Alex nodded and slowly made his way down the bumpy dirt path leading away from Seamus' cottage. "She reminded me this morning she'd drive straight to your place from school."

Twenty minutes later, Alex, Grant, Christine, Merlin Sage,

Needles, and I were crammed inside an interview room at the sheriff's station.

"My client still maintains her innocence," Merlin Sage said.

"Let's go over this one more time," Alex said.

For the next thirty minutes, Alex grilled Christine about the night of the murder, the murder weapon and hair found at the scene, her fingerprints, and her connection to Doc Drago, Marta Drago, and Greta Twinkle.

And Christine's answers never changed.

"At this point, Sheriff," Merlin Sage said, "you either have to arrest my client or let her go."

I closed my eyes. Those were not the words we wanted to hear. With the evidence we had against Christine, Alex would have no choice but to arrest her. I knew having worked at the Paranormal Apprehension and Detention Agency for over fifteen years that Alex could delay calling and having someone pick Christine up for twenty-four hours. After that, with the amount of physical evidence we had on Christine, she would be taken away, stripped of her fairy powers, and thrown into prison for the rest of her life.

There was no parole or second chances in the paranormal world when you were found guilty of murder.

Alex stood and nodded to Grant.

Clearing his throat and pushing himself off the wall, Grant walked over to Christine and helped her stand. "Christine Mossman, you're under arrest for the murder of Greta Twinkle. You have the right to remain silent…"

Christine Mossman openly wept as Grant led her from the interview room.

14

"You know what I just realized?" I looked up from the police report and pictures taken ten years ago after the vehicular accident. "We've spoken to Marta's best friend…but we've never spoken to Lena's best friend."

Alex stood, walked over to the coffeepot, and poured himself another cup. "That's because Marta's best friend, Christine Mossman, is supposedly the person responsible for taking revenge and killing Greta Twinkle."

"And hearing you say that statement out loud," I said, "tells me how ridiculous it now seems for Christine Mossman to be the killer."

"I have to agree," Grant said. "Our other suspects have more motive for wanting revenge than Christine does."

"I know it's what we think," Alex said, "but what can we prove?" He shook his head and sighed. "And our job isn't to *prove* Christine is innocent. Our own investigation has led us to Christine."

I held up my hand. "Just hear me out. What harm can come

from talking to Lena's bestie? I mean, maybe she can clear up the whole grocery store time lapse. Maybe after going to the grocery store and buying groceries, Lena stopped by to see her best friend? That's where she was for the missing hour and a half?"

Alex nodded. "You're right. We need to make sure we've answered all the questions before PADA comes and takes Christine away."

I stood and grabbed my cell phone off Grant's desk. "Who wants to take a trip to see Lena's best friend?"

"Do we even know who she is?" Grant asked. "From what you've said about Lena's husband, Bernard, he's not just going to hand over Lena's best friend's name."

"Please, that's what I have Mom and GiGi for." I pulled up Mom's contact information. "Mom'll know who Lena's best friend was."

Ten minutes later, Alex, Needles, and I were armed not only with the name of Lena's friend, but also an address, thanks to Mom and GiGi. Grant was on his way over to talk to Lena's niece one more time.

Bleu Faeman lived fifteen miles east of town, deep in the forest. We ended up having to ditch Alex's Blazer and walk the thirty feet to Bleu's magnificent cabin and fairy garden.

"These winter flowers are amazing." I stopped to admire the winter pansies, snowdrops, and snapdragons lining the walkway and hanging from pots from the front porch. "Absolutely beautiful."

"Thank you."

I spun around and saw a petite woman dressed in a sage green frock and black leggings. Her dainty hands were wrapped around a mug of steaming liquid.

"Good afternoon," I said. "I'm Shayla Loci, and this is

Sheriff Stone. We'd like to come in and ask you a couple questions, if we could?"

"Mercy, yes." She pushed open the screen door with her elbow. "I know you, child. Your mother and I exchange herbs for spells sometimes. And looky here…is that the famous Needles everyone talks about?"

Needles leaped off my shoulder, his wings glowing purple and silver, and gave a flourishing bow.

"Such a surprise to have you all here today," Bleu went on as she ushered us into her cluttered kitchen. There were spell jars lining the countertops and recessed shelves, and dried herbs and flowers hung from the ceiling. "Can I get you some hot tea? I just made my favorite, vanilla chamomile. I grow the chamomile and vanilla beans myself."

"I'd love a cup," I said.

Alex smiled as he sat down. "I could probably use some chamomile as well. I've had three cups of coffee today."

Bleu chuckled and poured us each a cup of tea, setting them down in front of us. She then strolled over to a cabinet, took out a handful of pretzels, and covered them in honey. "I've also heard about Needles' love of salty and sweet."

"I could kiss her." Needles flew down next to the plate on the counter, his wings glowing green and yellow, and devoured the snack.

"He says thank you," I said.

A tuxedo cat, who had been lounging in a ray of sunshine streaming through the windows, stood and stretched.

"That's Thistle," Bleu said.

Smiling, I reached down and scratched him under the chin. I closed my eyes and opened myself up to the cat. "He's happy and lazy." I grinned and opened my eyes. "But he could use a little treat as well."

Bleu laughed. "He's a good mouser." Bleu stood and opened the French doors. "Go on now, Thistle. Go earn your keep."

Meowing, the cat swished his tail, lifted his chin in the air, and strolled outside.

"I remember hearing about your ability," Bleu said. "You can sense the emotions of plants and animals, correct?"

"Yes. And sometimes I can even physically hear what they say."

"That's quite a gift you have." She took a sip of her tea. "Now tell me, why is it you three are here?"

"It's about Lena Craft," I said, "and everything that's going on in town."

Bleu set her mug down and nodded. "I received a call this morning from Luella Woods. She filled me in on what she knew about Christine Mossman getting arrested for killing someone." She smiled. "We fairies need to stick together. But I'm not sure what that woman's death has to do with Lena Craft. Lena's been gone for ten years now."

"Christine Mossman has been accused of killing Greta Twinkle," Alex said. "Greta was casually dating Doc Drago."

Bleu's eyes widened. "Really? I didn't realize."

"That's not the most astonishing part," I said. "When I found Greta's body, a note had been pinned to her. It referenced getting revenge for the death of Marta and Lena."

Bleu's hand flew to her mouth. "Oh, goddess above. Who would do something like that? I mean, I can't imagine Christine Mossman doing that. She's a little selfish and overly dramatic, but she's no cold-blooded killer."

"That's why we're here," Alex said. "We are hoping you might be able to shed some light on the accident."

"Me? What can I help with?"

"Lena's husband, Bernard, said Lena was coming home from

visiting her mother the night she was killed. She stopped to pick up some groceries and then drove home." I took a drink of my tea. "This is delicious, by the way."

Bleu gave me a small smile. "Thank you. And that's correct. I spoke to Lena around two on the day she died, and that's what she told me as well." Bleu looked over my shoulder, not quite meeting my eyes. "She was going to visit her mom, and then she needed to run by the store on the northwest side of the island and pick up a few things for the Valentine's Day dinner she was preparing the next night for Bernard."

I tilted my head to meet her gaze. "And that's what's bothering me. I know this island, Ms. Faeman. I grew up here. Things never change. The grocery store on the northwest side of the island closes at eight."

Bleu dropped her eyes and took a sip of her tea…her hands shaking. "I guess so."

"So where was Lena from eight until nine-thirty?" I asked softly, not wanting to spook her.

Bleu closed her eyes and sighed. "I had hoped no one would ever ask me that question."

"It's vital to our investigation," Alex said. "We really need to understand everything about the night Marta and Lena died."

Bleu nodded. "I never said anything because no one ever questioned why Lena was out that late. Not even her husband." She let out a small, breathy snort. "Which is probably a good thing."

"Where was she?" I prompted.

"Lena was seeing someone else."

I stared at Alex in stunned silence. For some reason, my mind hadn't even gone there. I guess because of how besotted Bernard seemed to be with Lena—dressing up the skeletons and all that—I just assumed Lena felt the same way about Bernard.

But then again, you know what they say when you assume something.

"Well, I didn't see that coming." Needles licked his paw. *"Did you, Princess?"*

"Who?" I asked. "Who was Lena seeing?"

Bleu shook her head. "I honestly don't know. She wouldn't tell me."

"You were her best friend," I said. "Do you really think we—"

"I'm telling you the truth," Bleu said sharply. "I tried to get her to tell me who he was, but she said it was still new, and she wanted to savor that for herself. When things progressed, she'd let me know." Bleu shrugged. "But she died before she could ever tell me."

"Do you have a guess?" Alex asked.

Needles snorted. *"Anyone would be better than that weirdo husband of hers."*

"I don't have a guess," Bleu said. "I mean, I always assumed it was someone who lived on the west or northwest side of the island, since she used her mother as cover. She'd tell Bernard she was going to see her Mom, and she would, but then she'd stop by and see this mystery man of hers."

"So on the night Lena died," I said, "she saw her mom, and she stopped by the grocery store, but then she also went to see this mystery man. That's why there's over an hour discrepancy in her timeline?"

Bleu nodded. "Yes. I'd say that's right. It's what I've always believed, anyway."

Alex frowned. "And you believe Bernard had no idea?"

"I know he didn't know," Bleu said. "Bernard is…well, let's just say he's a little unbalanced. If he even had an inkling Lena was cheating on him, he'd have gone ballistic."

"Crazier than he is now?" Needles picked up another pretzel. *"No way is that possible."*

"Have you seen how he lives now?" I asked.

Bleu snorted. "You mean with the entire legion of Lenas he has running around the house? Yeah, I've seen. It only took me stopping by once after Lena died to know I never wanted to visit him again." She pushed her mug away. "Don't be fooled by his reasons for the skeletons. It's not because he misses Lena so much. He needs someone to take care of him. The attachment to Lena was the excuse Bernard needed. He loved the way Lena took care of him more than he loved Lena. That's why she went looking for love."

15

"That was way more information than I thought we'd get from Bleu," I said once we were back inside the Blazer. "I would have never guessed Lena was with another man the night she died."

"Me neither." Needles settled down in his seat, yawned, then wrapped his wings around his body. *"I'm in need of a nap after all that food."*

"So looking at our three suspects," I said, "who lives on that side of the island?"

"You mean two suspects," Alex said. "I think we can rule out she was having an affair with her own husband."

I smacked my forehead with my hand. "Duh."

"So that leaves us with Howard and Seamus," Alex said.

"And we know for a fact Howard Wandman lives on that side of the island," I said. "In fact, now that we've read the report, I'm pretty sure he only lives about three miles from where the accident happened."

"We also know he's a playboy of sorts," Alex said. "He admitted to being married three times."

"He sure did." I turned to Alex, excitement running through me. "So are we going to go ask him if he was having an affair with Lena Craft the night she died?"

"I don't think so. You and I both know he'll just deny it. We need to find a way to link the affair and Lena's subsequent death to Howard Wandman's motive to lie in wait ten years before seeking revenge for Lena's death."

"We know Howard hates Doc," I said. "He's always seen him as competition. Not only did Doc take Marta away from Howard, but ultimately in the end, Marta took Lena away from Howard—if that's indeed who she was having the affair with. The only person Howard can blame is Doc. So for ten years, Howard plotted his revenge."

"But what if Doc hadn't been seeing anyone?" Alex asked. "What would Howard have done then?"

I shrugged. "Outright try to kill Doc?"

"Could be. I think the fact Greta Twinkle had the misfortune to date both Howard and Doc was her undoing. The fact she preferred Doc to Howard was the last straw for Howard. That was all the reason he needed to kill Greta on the ten-year anniversary."

"So now what?" I asked.

"We need some kind of proof. This is all just speculation on our part. We don't even have any circumstantial evidence."

"Okay, well, we know Howard was once married to Christine Mossman, right? When you think about all the parties involved, Howard has basically gotten revenge on everyone that has ever done him wrong. Isn't that enough proof?"

"No. Christine's fingerprints and hair are on the murder

weapon and at the scene of the crime. We need physical proof tying Howard to the murder."

"So now what?" I asked.

"Text Deputy Sparks. Tell him to sit on Howard Wandman tonight when he clocks in. If a call comes in through dispatch, he's to answer it, but I want him to stop patrolling the island around nine and just sit on Howard the rest of the night until maybe two or three in the morning."

"You think Howard might try something?"

"I'm not sure. I think he knows we're on to him, so I wouldn't put it past him to try something to divert our attention."

"Of course, the other two suspects know we're on to them as well."

Alex nodded and turned toward town. "That's true. But I think Howard is the one we need to focus on."

I sent Sparks a text and got an immediate response.

"Sparks said no problem, he'd stakeout Howard's place tonight."

"Good. Then I guess that's all we can do for right now."

"That was a nice cat nap," Needles said from the backseat. *"You sure we don't need to do a stakeout tonight, Princess? I could probably stay up."*

I laughed. "I think we can let Deputy Sparks handle it tonight." I looked at Alex. "Why don't you drop Needles and me off at my Bronco. I need to check out the southeast side of the island before I go home. A couple days ago, I noticed some weird drag marks down by the water. I want to make sure no one is poaching on the land down there."

"Be careful," Alex said.

"She's got me, Gargoyle," Needles said through a yawn. *"We'll be fine."*

* * *

"What do you think?" I asked Needles as I bent down to trace the weird drag marks. "They are too narrow for it to be an animal being dragged, but it's also not a body drag."

"Definitely not an animal. I don't think I've ever seen anything like it before."

"And why does it look like there's something solid in between the drag marks?"

I stood and looked around. This small section of the island was flat, unlike the rocky cliffs most of the island was made of. It was so flat, the thick forest and the ocean were only twenty feet away from each other. The tracks went from the water to the thick foliage behind me, but I couldn't tell if whatever was dragged came *out* of the ocean and went into the forest…or if it came out of the forest and went down to the ocean.

"There are no animals around," I said. "I can't talk to anyone to see if they've noticed anything odd."

"Kind of unusual," Needles said, his wings glowing gray and yellow. A sure sign he was worried. *"Where are all the woodland creatures?"*

"I'll come back again in a few days," I said. "Maybe I can find an animal to talk to then."

16

"So what do you think it is?" Alex ask as he and I sat in my kitchen drinking margaritas and watching Zoie cook.

"I have no idea," I said. "But I'll go back in a couple days and see if I can find any more tracks."

"Enough with the weird dragging thing," Zoie said, stirring the taco meat. "Let's talk about something exciting—like the wedding!"

I laughed. "What about it?"

Zoie rolled her eyes. "Hello! Let's talk about when, who will be in it, and again, *when*!"

"I got nothing," Needles said as he flew into the kitchen. *"None of the books in the library touch on an animal that could leave those kinds of markings."*

"We aren't talking about that anymore, Needles," Zoie said. "We're talking about the wedding."

Needles landed on the counter next to my arm. *"That so? Okay, so when is it?"*

"Would you guys stop hounding Shayla," Alex said. "It will be whenever she decides."

I leaned over and kissed him. "Thank you. I'm not ready yet to set a date." I held out my ring finger and examined the exquisite ring Alex had given me. "I'm still basking in the engagement."

Zoie turned to the cabinets and waved her hand, using magic to get down the plates. "Are we eating at the kitchen nook or dining room?"

"Let's eat here in the nook," I said. "Tacos should be feasted on in a casual setting."

Laughing, Zoie waved her hand again, and the plates settled down on the small table with the built-in bench window seating.

I reached over and snatched a pinch of shredded cheese and gobbled it up. "Need any help?"

"Nope. You and Dad just sit there and not talk about the wedding."

I grinned. "She's so subtle."

Dinner was amazing. It always was when I didn't have to cook. Alex and I cleaned up, while Zoie and Needles went to stoke the fire in the library. After our Monday night meal, we always ended up in the library reading and talking before bed.

"You know you can take all the time you need, right?" Alex said as he set the dried plate in the cabinet. "No one is really expecting you to set a date right now."

"I know." I picked up my margarita and downed the last of it. "But I've been giving it some thought."

"Really? Care to enlighten me?"

I grinned. "Soon."

We finished washing and drying, then snuggled up on the sofa in front of the library's fireplace. I spent most of the night thumbing through a magazine while Alex read the latest spy novel from one of his favorite supernatural authors. Zoie was texting friends on her phone, and Needles had retired upstairs to his bed—my old baby cradle.

Zoie yawned. "I'm ready for bed."

"Me too." I set down my magazine. "You ready, Alex?"

Alex placed a bookmark in the book and nodded.

"You know," Zoie said coyly. "Now that you two are *official* and all, you don't have to keep sleeping in two separate bedrooms." She rolled her eyes. "It's not like I'm a baby. I know what goes—"

"Stop!" Alex cried. "Do not finish that sentence." He shuddered. "I can't think about you being grown up enough to talk about such stuff."

Zoie rolled her eyes, and I laughed.

"Seriously, Dad? You're about four years too late with that worry."

Alex reached out and wrapped his arm around Zoie's neck and pulled her close. "Let me at least pretend."

"And Alex and I are perfectly fine sleeping in separate rooms," I said.

I didn't add as we all walked up the stairs that I'd been sleeping alone—for the most part—for forty years and was a little apprehensive about sharing a bed with someone now for the rest of my life.

I hugged Zoie and kissed Alex goodnight before shutting my bedroom door behind me. Shucking my game warden uniform, I donned a t-shirt and warm fuzzy lounge pants and crawled into bed.

I wasn't sure how long I'd been asleep, but the next thing I remember, my eyes flew open and I sat up in bed. My heart was racing, but I couldn't figure out what was wrong! I was about to scramble out of bed when the house started to shake.

Throwing back the covers, I sprang out of bed and threw open my bedroom door. Zoie and Alex were also stumbling into the hallway.

"What's going on?" Zoie yelled as the ground rumbled again.

"It's Black Forest King," Needles said as he zipped over to where we stood, his wings glowing a reddish-gray with worry. *"He's angry. Something is wrong with—it's Serenity! He's letting me know through our link that your mother is distressed and scared. She needs our help now!"*

"Mom? Mom's in trouble?"

I ran to grab my phone off my nightstand, and at the same time, I heard Alex's phone ring. I snatched my cell phone and called Mom.

No answer.

I ran back out into the hallway. "She's not answering!"

"I just got a call from dispatch," Alex said. "There's a fire at your mom's house. That's all I know."

I staggered and fell against the wall. "Oh, my goddess. We need to get to her now!"

"I just informed Black Forest King we are on our way." I could hear the worry in Needles' voice, and that was nearly my undoing.

"What should I do?" Zoie asked.

"Fly down the lane to GiGi's cottage," Alex said. "Do you think you can fly her to Serenity's?"

Zoie nodded. "Yes. I'll go right now."

Not even bothering to change out of our pajamas, Alex and I ran down the stairs, Needles flying behind us. I yanked open the front door, and as we stepped out into the cool night, Alex shifted into his gargoyle form and Needles snuggled down inside my shirt. I was already shivering from the cold, but I pushed the discomfort away. I could always conjure up a jacket when we got to Mom's.

Scooping me up into his stone arms and being careful not to scratch me with his long, sharp talons, Alex shot up into the sky and headed toward town.

17

Alex set me down in Mom's front yard, then shifted back to his human form. Lights from all the emergency vehicles were flashing, but the sirens were off. As Needles flew out from my t-shirt, I quickly scanned the faces until I found Mom standing near her driveway. Crying out, I ran to her, and she enveloped me in a hug.

"Are you okay?" I demanded.

Still hugging, I felt Mom's head move against my shoulder. "I'm okay. And so is the house, for the most part. It was heavily warded, so the fire really didn't penetrate." She stepped back and turned toward her beloved house. "Looks like there's some damage to the roof, my front yard is burned to a crisp, and windows broke out." Mom pointed to her two flat tires. "Fire popped my car tires as well. Probably even some damage to the car. Luckily, Amara and two of her men contained the fire before it reached the other houses."

Amara Seawall was an elemental witch who could control

water. She'd been the town's fire chief for as long as I could remember.

"Thank the goddess you're okay," I said. "The house is just a house. We can fix it."

Zoie dropped from the sky and set GiGi down. The minute GiGi's feet touched the ground, she hobbled toward us. When she reached Mom, I took a step back so they could have a private moment and went to stand by Zoie.

"This is just awful," Zoie said.

"Hey," Serena said as she sidled up next to us. "Does your mom know what happened?"

I hugged Serena. "When did you guys get here?"

"Grant got the call about ten minutes ago," Serena said. "We knew something had to be wrong because we woke up to our house shaking. After Grant told me about the call from dispatch, I called Mom and let her know, and she insisted on coming too."

Sure enough, Aunt Starla and the former sheriff, Walt Hawkins, were standing next to Alex and Grant. "I haven't had a chance to ask Mom if she knows how the fire started. I wanted to give her and GiGi a moment."

"I think the whole island felt the rumble," Needles said. *"Black Forest King was scared and angry."*

"I knew your dad was powerful, Shayla," Zoie said, "but it's crazy to think he could make this whole island shake. I mean, it's a huge island." Her brow furrowed. "And I don't understand how he could do something like that."

"Dad is a genius loci," I said. "He literally embodies Black Forest, which is a part of the island. Therefore, *Dad* is a part of the island."

"Wow, and I thought it was cool my dad could turn into a gargoyle and fly."

I laughed despite my anxiety over Mom. "Yeah, my dad is pretty special."

A few minutes later, GiGi and Mom walked over to where Serena, Zoie, Needles, and I stood.

"Do you know what happened, Mom?" I asked.

"I think Alex and Grant need to be here," Mom said. "They're gonna want to hear this."

I motioned for Alex, Grant, Aunt Starla, and Walt to come over. When Aunt Starla got close, she nearly tackled Mom to the ground. The two clung to each other and cried.

"Do you know how this happened, Serenity?" Alex asked once Mom and Aunt Starla let go of each other.

Mom nodded. "Someone set it. The fire was from the outside trying to come in."

"You're sure?" Alex asked.

"Yes. I awoke to the fire alarms going off, and I immediately sent out a pulse of magic to find out where the fire was located. When Mom and I warded this house nearly twenty years ago, we warded it against fire and theft. Since my magic couldn't detect anything from the inside, I knew it had to be from the outside trying to come in. There's no other explanation." Mom pointed to the roof. "And if you look at the house, you'll notice that there's nothing wrong with the inside. It's all on the outside. My roof looks scorched, my front yard is dead, and a couple windows have been blown out. But that's all."

I blew out a ragged breath, anger coursing through my body. "So someone deliberately set fire to your house?"

Mom nodded. "Yes."

I looked at Needles. "I need you to communicate to Dad that Mom is okay."

"Already done, Princess." Needles dropped to my shoulder. *"That's why there's no more earthquake. He's furious, though,*

and wants to know for himself Serenity is okay. The stubborn Black Forest King won't take my word for it."

Amara strolled over to us. "I think we got it all under control now, Serenity. Luckily, it's only the outside that's water logged. We took care where the windows were broken out. You shouldn't have much water damage inside." She frowned. "When I come back out in the morning and have better light, I'll be able to tell more…but right now, I'd say the fire was started in the bushes by your window."

"Why would someone do that?" Aunt Starla demanded.

"It's a statement," I said.

Amara shoved her hands in her pants pockets. "I don't have to tell you, Serenity, that you can't stay here tonight. Like I said, I want my men and me to come back in the morning when it's light and take another look around." Amara smiled at Mom. "I know you have plenty of places to stay, so I'll get out of here. I'm sorry this happened, but it could have been a lot worse, Serenity."

I waited until Amara left before rounding on Alex. "I think we made our killer nervous, and now they're trying to pull our focus in a different direction."

Mom scoffed. "Well, the killer is dumb. He or she doesn't know who they're messing with. This is just gonna make you guys even more determined to find out who killed Greta Twinkle."

"And I think it's safe to say," I said, "it wasn't Christine Mossman."

"If you need my help," Walt Hawkins said, "just let me know."

Alex nodded. "I know you're gonna come by the station in the morning. That would be a big help. Shayla and I found out something today that may interest you regarding the death of Lena Craft."

Walt's eyebrows rose in surprise. "I'll be at the station by ten."

Alex looked around. "Dozens of neighbors out on their lawns. Grant, why don't you and Serena take the left side over here, and Shayla and I will take the right side. Somebody had to have seen something."

"Alex," Mom said gently, "it's almost one in the morning. Who on earth would have seen what happened?"

Alex wrapped an arm around Mom's shoulder and pulled her close, kissing her temple. "You never know, Serenity. We just may find a witness."

"Where are you going to stay?" I asked mom.

"With me," Aunt Starla and GiGi both said.

Mom laughed. "I know it's late, but I really would like to go see Black Forest King. I know he's worried."

"I could fly you there," Zoie offered.

"Take my car, Serenity," Aunt Starla said. "You and GiGi need a vehicle until yours can get fixed. Someone here can take Walt and me back to my place."

Alex turned to Zoie. "Why don't you go back to our place and stay in town? No sense flying back out to the castle tonight. I'll be home when I finish up here."

"You sure?" Zoie mused.

Alex nodded.

"Can Needles stay with me?" Zoie asked in a small voice.

"Of course," I said. "Needles, you don't mind staying with Zoie, do you?"

Needles' wings turned green. He clicked his bottom paws together and gave me a salute. *"I'd be honored to watch over Miss Zoie, Princess."*

❧ 18 ❧

Ten minutes later, exhausted and frustrated, Alex and I stopped in front of our last house. Not a single person we'd spoken to had seen or heard anything…not until the emergency vehicles arrived, anyway.

Grant had texted and said the same thing. No luck on his side of the street. Alex told him and Serena to go on home, and we'd start again in the morning.

And the bad news kept on rolling in.

Deputy Sparks called Alex to inform him Howard Wandman had been home the entire night. Sparks watched Howard go upstairs and turn off his bedroom light around eleven, then turn it on again around twelve-fifteen when the island started to shake. Once the rumbling stopped, Howard turned off his light and went back to sleep.

We were at our last house with no answers to who tried to set Mom's house on fire. Dispatch had informed Alex that the island's equivalent to a 911 call had come from a cell phone pinging from this house.

"I can't believe no one saw anything," I mumbled.

"We've still got this house," Alex said. "And supposedly the emergency call came from here. So maybe we'll get lucky."

We ambled up the sidewalk to the two-story brick house. I was surprised to see a girl, no older than nineteen or twenty, sitting on the front porch drinking something hot.

"Hello," Alex said. "I'm Sheriff Stone, and this Shayla Loci."

The girl lifted her hand in greeting, but didn't say anything.

"Can we ask you a few questions?" I asked. "It's my mom's house that was on fire."

The girl nodded. "Yeah. Is Miss Serenity okay?"

"Mom's fine…thank you for asking."

"I nearly had a heart attack when I saw the flames," the girl said.

"What's your name?" Alex asked.

"Missy Stoneblock."

"You're a gargoyle?" Alex asked, surprise ringing in his voice.

The girl shrugged. "I dunno. I guess so." She snorted and looked away. "Not sure how much of a gargoyle I am, considering I can't fly." She turned back and scrutinized Alex with her young, knowing eyes. "I hear you and your daughter can shift to stone *and* fly. That's pretty cool. I can only make my skin hard. I wish I could fly." She snorted. "I mean, what kind of gargoyle am I really?"

"A good one," Alex said. "I'm sure you know gargoyles are protectors, and from what we've discovered tonight, you did just that by calling for help. So if you're asking me? I'd say you're the perfect kind of gargoyle."

The girl sat up straighter. "Really? You think so?"

"I know so," Alex said. "Being a gargoyle isn't defined by

your ability to fly." He tapped his heart. "It's about caring and protecting those around you."

"I guess I never thought about it like that." She gave Alex a small smile. "Thanks. Of course, I still wish I could fly."

Alex chuckled. "It *is* pretty cool. What can you tell us about what happened tonight?"

The girl took a sip of her drink. "I'd just gotten home because my curfew is midnight." The girl rolled her eyes. "Since I still live with my parents, they think I need a curfew, even though I'm an adult. I swear, this island needs more housing! I have two girlfriends who'd move in with me right now if we could just find a place." She waved her hand in the air. "But anyway, I was at my front door when I turned and saw someone running from Miss Serenity's yard. A few seconds later, I saw the smoke and could smell the fire. I ran inside and called the fire department." She shook her head. "And then I *really* freaked when I came back outside and the ground started to shake! I still don't understand why that happened. I didn't know we could get earthquakes on Enchanted Island."

I didn't bother to tell her it was my dad in a fit of rage and panic. No sense getting the locals in a panic as well.

"But you saw someone fleeing?" Alex asked.

"Yeah." The girl shrugged again. "I mean, it was dark. Only the streetlights overhead to give off light, so I can't be sure of what I saw, but I think it was a woman. She was wearing a dress, and I could see it billing behind her as she ran. She was going in the opposite direction, so I never saw her face or anything."

"This helps," I said.

"And remember what I said about being a gargoyle," Alex said. "You are not defined by the wings, you are defined by your character. And you showed plenty of it tonight."

Tears filled the girl's eyes. "Thanks. I'm almost finished with my classes to be a certified medical technician. Hopefully, I'll be able to serve the island that way soon."

Alex nodded. "I will put in a good word for you when the time comes."

Missy grinned. "You're all right, Sheriff Stone."

We thanked her and headed back toward Mom's.

"What the heck is going on here?" I mused.

"Christine Mossman is still in custody, so it can't be her Missy just saw running from the house. Our main suspect, Howard, has been home all night. So what woman is doing this?"

"It's going to sound insane," Alex said, pausing in front of the fire truck, "but I really think we need to haul in Bernard Craft, Lena's husband. We know for a fact he has dresses from when Lena was alive. At this point, I seriously wouldn't put it past him to animate the skeletons for evil." He turned to look at me. "And I can't believe I just said those words out loud."

I laughed. "Yeah, this case just keeps getting weirder and weirder."

I nearly jumped out of my skin when the ambulance siren blasted and filled the air…then shot down the street seconds later.

"What's that about?" I mused.

Alex's cell phone rang. "This is Sheriff Stone. What? Where? His house? We'll be right there."

"What's going on?" I demanded when Alex disconnected.

"It's Doc Drago," Alex said. "He's been shot."

19

Alex shifted, and together we flew toward Doc Drago's house. We'd just touched down in the yard as the paramedics raced inside.

Doc was sitting on a barstool in his kitchen, arguing good-naturedly with a woman. I didn't recognize her, but she was dressed in scrubs.

"And you're sure you finished medical school, Meridia?" Doc asked. "Because this sure does hurt."

The paramedics grinned at each other…but all took a step backward.

"I swear, Drago, if you don't stop complaining…" The woman didn't finish her sentence. Instead, she placed her hand over Doc's open wound and whispered something under her breath. A few seconds later, a bullet emerged from Doc's shoulder.

"You were shot?" Alex asked.

"Yep. I woke up to my house shaking, and then a few minutes later, I could hear sirens in the distance. Not something you normally hear on Enchanted Island, so I got up to see what was going on. I looked out my bedroom window but couldn't see anything."

Meridia cast a healing spell over Doc's shoulder, then placed a bandage over the open wound.

"By that time, I was up and knew I wouldn't be able to fall back asleep, so I went into the kitchen here to make me some hot milk. Probably took all of five or ten minutes. I was standing by the window over there drinking and listening in to the emergency scanner to see where the sirens had stopped, when I heard a *crack*...and then seconds later felt pain in my shoulder."

"Did you see anyone outside?" Alex asked.

"I didn't see a soul. It didn't even register with me I'd been shot until I noticed the glass was shattered and there was pain in my left shoulder."

"My shift at the hospital ends at midnight," Meridia said. "I was just getting out of my car when I heard the gunshot. I couldn't tell what direction the shot came from, so I did a locator spell to find out who was injured and bleeding within a two-block area. Doc here popped up on my radar."

"Is your mom okay?" Doc asked. "I'd just heard the emergency vehicles were all at Serenity's address when I was shot."

"Mom's fine," I said. "So is her house." I glanced at Alex. "I guess now we know why the killer tried to burn down Mom's house—he needed a distraction. This way, he was free to come over here and shoot Doc, his intended target."

"But why wouldn't the person just burn down Doc's house?" a paramedic asked.

"They needed me incapacitated," Doc said. "House fire, I could shift and fly and search them out that way. With a bullet inside me, I'd have to wait to have it removed before I could shift. If I shifted with a bullet inside me, it would stay inside me."

Alex nodded. "So whoever shot you knows that much about shifters."

"We just heard," Grant said as he and Serena ran into the kitchen. "Anything we can do?"

"Dr. Witchazel just pulled out my slug," Doc said.

"Do you think you can drop it by the forensic lab on your way home?" Alex asked.

"Of course," Grant said.

I closed my eyes, conjured up an evidence bag using my magic, then levitated the bullet into the bag.

"Great," Alex said. "We at least have a bullet to match to the gun."

"You okay, Doc?" Serena asked.

"I'll be fine," Dr. Drago said. "Dragons heal quickly. That's why it was important to get the bullet out before the wound closed."

"Why don't you let Serena and me help you canvas the area real quick," Grant said. "Meet back up in thirty?"

Alex nodded. "That would be a big help. Thanks you guys."

After thirty exhausting minutes, no one had anything new to report.

"What's next?" Grant asked.

"We go home," Alex said. "We can start back up in the morning."

I nodded. "Serena, you have to be at the bakery in just a couple hours. You need some sleep."

Serena grinned. "I can make some strong coffee in the morning, Shayla. Don't worry about me."

"Deputy Sparks said Howard Wandman never left his house

tonight," Alex said. "I think we need to press Bernard Craft and Seamus Oakleaf. I believe the answer lies with one of them."

"I'll pick up Bernard first," Grant said. "If that works for you? Bring him down to the station for a formal interview."

Alex nodded. "Sounds good."

Once Grant and Serena were gone, I called Mom to let her know about Doc Drago.

"I just came from seeing your father," Mom said. "He's calmed down, but I wouldn't want to be in the shoes of the bad guy right now. Your father is not someone to cross."

"You staying at the castle tonight?"

"Yes," Mom said. "That's okay, right?"

I snorted. "Of course. You can stay there as long as you need to. There's plenty of space."

And it was true. Not only did we have the five bedrooms spaced out on the second floor, but Alex and Grant had recently dry walled the entire attic and put in a bathroom, so now I had even more living space.

"I'll see you in about ten minutes." I disconnected. "And before you ask, yes, you have to keep Needles overnight."

Sighing, Alex shifted and lifted me in his arms.

"It's a good thing I love you, Shayla Loci," he said, his voice deep and gravely from the shift. "Because the porcupine might have been a deal breaker."

20

Enchanted Bakery & Brew was packed when Alex, Needles, and I strolled inside early the next morning. It didn't take long to realize everyone was talking about the fire and Doc being shot.

"I just don't understand what's going on anymore," Gladys Thyme said. "It used to be this island was safe. Now I'm not so sure."

I reached down and squeezed Alex's hand. It wasn't his fault, but I knew he felt the pressure.

"Sheriff, what are you going to do to ensure our safety?" Pepper Leafton asked.

"The same thing I've been doing since the day I got here," Alex said. "Make sure I do everything I can to protect the citizens of Enchanted Island."

"Let the gargoyle be!" GiGi's voice rang out. "Many of you don't want to look in the mirror, because if you did, you'd see family members who have recently been arrested because of their disturbing behavior. None of this is the sheriff's fault. Before you throw your stones, check yourselves!"

There were murmurs of "sorry" and eyes being averted as Alex and I strolled over to the display case. How quickly supernaturals could turn. Yesterday, everyone was excited and wanted to see my ring and ask about the wedding…today, the fear had taken hold and panic had set in.

"Leave it to GiGi to set everyone straight," Needles said.

"The usual? Serena asked.

"Yes," I said. "And make my coffee the largest you got."

"I'll bring it to you," Serena said. "Go on and find a seat with Mom and Aunt Serenity."

"Don't forget my caramel salt stick," Needles said, his wings glowing green. *"Something tells me I'm gonna need it."*

Serena laughed. "You got it, Needles."

Alex and I pushed our way through the crowd and stopped in front of the table where Mom, GiGi, Aunt Starla, and Walt Hawkins sat. Two chairs suddenly appeared at our sides, and Alex and I sat as well.

"You still need me to stop by the station this morning?" Walt asked.

Alex nodded. "That would be great. We are questioning two suspects, but after that, I'd love to talk with you."

Walt leaned over the table. "You really think there's a connection between Greta Twinkle's murder and the accident that happened ten years ago?"

Alex nodded. "I do."

"Then I'll see you at the station in a couple hours."

Tamara strolled over with our coffees and cinnamon rolls to go. She patted Alex on the shoulder. "Don't listen to what anyone says. You're fabulous at your job. Everyone who works for you is good at their job."

"Thank you, Tamara," Alex said.

"Well, we better head out." I stood and grabbed the white bag that held our goodies, while Alex grabbed the coffees. "Will you be around later today, Mom?"

Mom nodded. "Stop by whenever you can."

The crowd parted for Alex and me as we headed to the front door. Nobody tried to stop us or ask us what our plans were for the day. I figured it was because most people were too scared to say anything with GiGi still in the bakery.

Making sure my precious Bronco was locked up tight and still heavily warded, I followed Alex to his Blazer. Needles slipped to the back when I opened the door and hopped inside.

"I'm making a judgment call to release Christine Mossman this morning," Alex said. "As you know, I have to call the Paranormal Apprehension and Detention Agency within twenty-four hours of detainment for murder. My twenty-four hours are coming to a close, and with all that's happened, I just can't do it. I'm not convinced Christine is the killer, no matter how much evidence is piled against her."

I snapped on my seatbelt. "I agree. If I were in your shoes, I'd make the same call."

Opal Earthly-Caraway was behind her desk when we strolled inside the sheriff's station. The octogenarian's wrinkled skin glowed copper from her days out in the Hawaiian sun.

"Did you do a lot of bungee jumping?" I asked.

Opal grinned. "Bungee jumping, cliff diving, parasailing, and more fruity rum drinks than I can count."

"Sounds like paradise," I said.

"It was. But I hear you guys have had quite the mystery while I was away."

"We have."

Opal grinned. "I could hear Christine Mossman wailing from

my desk out here when I arrived this morning. She sure can make a fuss."

Grant motioned us over from his desk. "Finn texted me about ten minutes ago to let me know she saw the bullet in her lab this morning."

Alex nodded. "Good. Now, I want to tell you the same thing I just told Shayla. I'm making the judgment call to release Christine Mossman this morning. I don't believe she killed Greta Twinkle."

"I agree with that decision," Grant said. "We are obviously missing a key piece to this puzzle."

"Walt should be here in a couple hours," Alex said. "Hopefully, he can shed some light on this for us."

21

"That's it?" Christine demanded. "After all the questions and the night in jail, you're just letting me go free? I'm not sure if I'm relieved or livid."

"Maybe if you call your Valentine's date, you two can make it up tonight?" I suggested.

Christine patted her lacquered hair. "Well, I'll have to spend the day at the spa getting refreshed after my trauma of being incarcerated, but perhaps you're right." She ran her hands down her sides. "Maybe this guy likes a witch who's been in the slammer?"

"Oh, good grief," Needles grumbled from my shoulder.

I couldn't help the laugh that escaped. "Maybe so, Christine."

Grant returned to the sheriff's station soon after Christine left with Bernard Craft by his side.

"I don't understand why you had to drag me down here," Bernard said.

Grant continued to lead Bernard down the hallway to one of

the interview rooms, not even bothering to answer. Alex and I fell into step behind them.

The four of us sat down at the table while Needles perched on the back of my chair.

"I'm just gonna jump right in," Alex said. "We'd like to talk about your wife. Specifically, the night Lena died."

"Why?" Bernard snapped. "So you can see my pain?"

"I love it when the crazies get all dramatic," Needles said.

I had to look away so I wouldn't laugh out loud. It was especially hard to keep a straight face sometimes now that I knew others around me could hear Needles as well.

Alex folded his hands on the table. "You said your wife was on her way home from visiting her mom and running an errand at the grocery store. Is that correct?"

"Yes."

"Are you aware the grocery store she went to closes at eight o'clock?" Alex asked.

"So what? What does that have to do with anything?"

Alex leaned across the table. "We're all just wondering where your wife was between eight and nine-thirty."

Bernard's face turned red, and he narrowed his eyes. "How should I know? I guess if she were still alive, we could ask her."

"How was your marriage?" I asked. "Were you and Lena getting along the weeks leading up to her death?"

Bernard slammed his hand down on the table. "How dare you ask me a question like that! Of course my wife and I got along."

"He's lying," Needles said. *"I say we string him up and torture him a little. See what he has to say then."*

"Was your wife seeing another man?" I asked.

"Absolutely not!"

"So you deny your wife was having an affair?" Alex asked.

"Your damn right I'm denying it!" Bernard stood. "And I

refuse to sit here any longer while you trash my dead wife's name."

"Sit down, Mr. Craft," Grant said.

"I won't have you spreading lies about—"

"Detective Wolfe told you to sit down." There was enough force in Alex's tone, that Bernard immediately sat down.

Grant retrieved his small notebook from his pocket. "Mr. Craft, can you tell us where you were last night between midnight and one in the morning?"

"Why? What business is it of yours?"

"Just answer the question," Grant said smoothly.

"Not that it's any of your business, but I was in bed. Sleeping."

"Anyone who can corroborate that?" Grant asked.

"Just all those creepy skeletons," Needles muttered.

"Of course someone can verify my whereabouts," Bernard grumbled. "All of my Lenas were home."

"I refuse to go back to his house and question those skeletons!" Needles exclaimed, his wings glowing gray and black.

"Is there anyone *alive,"* Grant said, "who can verify your whereabouts?"

Bernard scowled. "No, no one alive."

"Do you own a gun?" Grant asked.

"A gun? No."

Grant shut his notebook, and Alex picked up on the cue.

"Thank you, Mr. Craft," Alex said. "That's all the questions we have for now. Grant will escort you back to your place."

Twenty-five minutes later, Grant walked through the door again, this time with Seamus Oakleaf at his side. Once again, Alex and I fell into step behind Grant as he escorted Seamus into the interview room.

"We just have a few questions for you," Alex said.

"If this has to do with what happened to Doc last night," Seamus said, "I already know. I don't normally pay attention to gossip, but one of my sister's friends from back when she was alive called to let me know what happened. I'm not sure why she thought I would care. I'd only care if whoever shot Doc had succeeded in killing him."

"This fairy has some serious hatred," Needles said.

I couldn't argue with him.

"This does have something to do with what happened to Doc," Alex said. "Can you tell us where you were between midnight and one o'clock last night?"

Seamus threw his hands up in the air. "You're serious? At that time of night, I was at home in bed. Exactly where I am every night. In case you missed it, I don't like to socialize. Why would I? Everything I ever loved was taken from me ten years ago. All because Doc couldn't be bothered to see the signs right in front of his face."

"You own a gun, Mr. Oakleaf?" Alex asked.

Seamus snorted. "A gun? No, of course not. If I have a problem, I solve it with magic... not a gun."

"Thank you for your time," Alex said. "Grant will see you back home."

Once Seamus Oakleaf and Grant were gone, I rested my head on the table. "Both of those men hate Doc, and both had opportunity and motive to hurt him."

"I know," Alex said.

"What if we're totally off here? What if we should be searching for a woman? That's who our witnesses believe they saw running from Greta's home *and* from Mom's place last night."

"But what woman?" Alex asked.

I lifted my head. "This may be a totally crazy theory, but what if it's the *wife* of whoever Lena was having an affair with?"

"I think that's definitely a possibility we need to look into," Alex said. "We just need to figure out who Lena was having an affair with."

I snorted. "That might be easier said than done."

A soft knock sounded on the door, and Walt Hawkins stood at the threshold.

"C'mon in, Walt," Alex said.

"I just saw Seamus Oakleaf and Grant leaving the station," Walt said. "He one of your suspects for Greta Twinkle's murder?"

I nodded. "Yep. Him and Bernard Craft."

Walt pulled out a chair, then lowered himself. "So you think either Bernard or Seamus killed Greta Twinkle? And it has to do with what happened the night Marta Drago and Lena Craft died?" He shook his head. "That's a big pill to swallow."

"Just hear us out," Alex said.

I nodded. "Alex and I believe if we can answer one question, it might help explain how all of this is connected."

"What's the question?"

"It's about the night Marta had her aneurysm and hit Lena Craft," I said. "Where was Lena coming from?"

Walt frowned. "If I'm not mistaken, she was driving back from visiting her mother, who lived on the northwest side of the island."

"And she made one stop after visiting her mother?" Alex asked.

"Yes. Bernard said Lena had to go to the grocery store to pick up some items. Why? What have you found out?"

Alex crossed his arms over his chest. "Shayla told me the

grocery store on the northwest side of the island closes at eight o'clock. Always has."

Walt nodded. "I guess that's right."

"From where Bernard and Lena lived on the southwest side of the island, to where the accident happened, it's only a fifteen minute drive from the grocery store."

"Okay," Walt said.

No one said anything for a full ten seconds, then Walt cursed. "Where was Lena that other hour?"

"That's what we've been trying to figure out," Alex said.

Walt shook his head. "How could I have missed this?"

"I'm sure at the time of the accident," I said, "emotions were high. No one thought to question what Bernard had said."

"So where was Lena?" Walt said. "Do you know?"

"Shayla and I spoke to Lena's best friend at the time, Bleu Faeman. She told us Lena was having an affair, but she doesn't know who the man was."

Walt whistled. "An affair? I can't believe I missed something so important, and I can't believe Lena Craft was having an affair and no one whispered about it either before or after her death."

I snorted. "Right? This is a small island when it needs to be. Gossip has a life of its own. If anyone knew about the affair, they'd have whispered it."

Walt furrowed his brows. "So you're thinking whoever Lena was sleeping with ten years ago may be the person behind who killed Greta Twinkle on the anniversary of Lena's death?"

Alex shrugged. "Something like that. The killer knows they can't hurt Marta because she's already dead, so they're going to hurt the next best thing—her husband. And how can they hurt Doc? By killing someone he's been seeing, even if it was just casual dating."

"That's convoluted and twisted," Walt said.

"The witnesses we've spoken to," I said, "have mentioned a woman fleeing the scene. So we're thinking it might be the *wife* of the man Lena was sleeping with. Maybe the man Lena was having an affair with left his wife after Lena's death? Or maybe the man Lena was having the affair with has recently died, giving the wife the catalyst she needed to start hurting others? I'm not really sure of the reason yet, but it's the best guess we have so far." I shrugged. "Then again, we could be off base, and it's either Bernard or Seamus."

"I wish I could help you," Walt said. "But I never heard anyone mention Lena stepping out on Bernard."

22

Alex, Needles, and I dropped by Mom's house for a late lunch and to see if she and GiGi knew anything about Lena having an affair. Before I'd left the castle this morning, Mom told me she and GiGi would be driving back into town to check out the house in the morning light.

Mom's house looked just as terrifying in the daylight as it did last night. Her yard was still scorched, but I could see patches of green scattered throughout the yard. GiGi must be trying to counteract the dead grass with a revive spell. It would take a few tries, but eventually the grass would be green again.

Sal Willow & Sons were installing new windows when Alex and I strolled inside Mom's house.

"The inside looks amazing," Alex said. "I can't believe the difference. Like there wasn't even a fire here last night."

I smiled. "Mom and GiGi know what they're doing when it comes to warding houses."

"Shayla? Is that you?" Mom's voice rang out.

"Yes. We thought we'd stop by for some lunch."

"And a pretzel," Needles added.

Mom and GiGi were sitting at the kitchen table drinking hot tea and eating cranberry-lemon scones.

"I just made chicken salad," Mom said. "I bought a batch of fresh croissants from the bakery this morning, so make yourselves a sandwich, and then have some cranberry-lemon scones for dessert."

"Praise Serena and her baking skills," I said.

"You got that right." GiGi shoved the last of her scone into her mouth and grinned.

Alex passed me the croissants, and I busied myself by stuffing the croissants with huge heaping spoonfuls of Mom's chicken salad. Once the sandwiches were done, I grabbed a handful of pretzels from a bag Mom kept on hand and handed them to Needles. Alex carried our milk to the table, and we sat down next to Mom and GiGi.

"The inside of the house looks amazing," Alex said. "You'd never know there was a fire here last night."

Mom nodded. "The ward held up nicely." Mom sent GiGi a look I couldn't interpret. "But even so, I'm thinking about making some improvements around here in the next few months."

I stopped chewing and put my sandwich down. "What kind of improvements?"

Mom shrugged and took a sip of her tea. "Nothing big. Just a few changes here and there."

"Change is always good," GiGi said.

I totally disagreed. Change wasn't always good, and I didn't like the way this sounded. But I knew better than to force the hand. Mom and GiGi would spill the beans when they thought the time was right.

"I have a question," I said. "At the time of Lena Craft's

death, did you two ever hear whispers about her having an affair with another man?"

Mom and GiGi both gaped at me.

"I never did," Mom said.

"Trust me, if that rumor had gotten around, I'd have heard about it," GiGi said. "You really think it's true? Lena Craft was having an affair with someone?"

Alex nodded. "It's a theory we are testing out."

GiGi reached for another scone. "Not to change the subject, but is Zoie still coming out to the cottage tonight? It's the full moon."

Alex nodded. "She'll be there. She's been talking about it for days now."

* * *

Alex pulled into the back parking lot of the sheriff's station. Doc was standing next to his vehicle—which was shaded by a huge oak tree. Doc turned around and waved with his good arm.

"Hey, Doc," I said. "What are you doing here? Shouldn't you be home resting?"

"I just came in real quick to check on a few things in the lab. I'm heading back home now."

"How is your shoulder feeling?" Alex asked.

"Feels like he got shot." Needles laughed and did a couple somersaults in the air, his wings glowing green and yellow.

"Shoulder is a little stiff," Doc said. "But by tomorrow, it should be back to normal. Like I said, dragons heal fairly quickly."

"You go home and rest," I said. "Holler if you need anything."

"Will do, Shayla."

Doc wrenched open his car door and slid behind the wheel. He'd started to back up when the oak tree in front of him groaned loudly, uprooted itself, and crashed down on Doc's car. For a few seconds, Alex, Needles, and I just stood there.

Then reality set in.

"Doc!" Alex shouted. "Can you hear us?"

The tree had landed atop Doc's vehicle, crushing the roof and the hood. The windows had shattered, and the glass lay strewn about the ground near our feet.

"I'm good," Doc ground out. "Stand back. I'm going to shift. I hope that will cause the metal to move enough so I can get out."

Alex and I backed up, while Needles flew higher in the air so he could look down on the mess. Seconds later, I heard the groan and creak of the metal as Doc shifted into his Dragon form. A huge claw with razor-sharp talons ripped off a chunk of metal and tossed it aside. Soon, Doc's dragon head poked out, and he slowly eased his scaled, mammoth body out of the twisted mess.

"Princess, do a locator spell," Needles hollered down from above us. *"See if you can get a read on anyone using magic."*

I close my eyes and opened myself up to everything around me. Myriad emotions slammed into me, and I had to quickly compartmentalize them. The poor oak tree that had fallen on Doc's car was in agony, but I had to push that aside for right now and see if I could get a read on anyone using magic around me. I could make out people shouting and running, but I didn't pick up on anyone using magic.

"Nothing," I hollered up to Needles. "They must be using a cloaking spell. Did you see anything?"

"No. Sorry, Princess." Needles settled back down on my shoulder, his wings glowing gray with worry.

The back door of the station flew open, and Grant, Finn,

Opal, and Pearl all rushed outside. Daisy Woods also rounded the corner and hurried over to us.

"I was walking by during my lunch," Daisy panted, "and I saw the tree fall."

Doc shifted back to his human form and staggered. Alex caught him around the shoulders and gently eased him to the ground.

"I got ambulances on the way," Grant said as he jogged over to where we all stood.

"Shayla," Needles said. *"They've got Doc, but you and Daisy need to get to the tree."*

For the first time, I took a good look at the oak tree that had fallen onto Doc's car. The roots were shattered and broken, huge chunks of bark were missing from the trunk, and branches were bent and hanging loose.

"A summoning spell," I whispered. "Someone forced the oak tree to uproot itself and try to kill Doc."

"We must get it replanted," Daisy said. "Otherwise, it will die."

I knew she and Needles were right. I could feel the tree crying out in agony. "The tree is under a lot of stress. I'm going to do a calming spell to help ease the torment. I need you, Daisy, to cover the roots to keep them from drying out."

Daisy quickly shed her sweater, bent down, and carefully wrapped the exposed roots. I closed my eyes, reached out and touched the oak tree's trunk, and whispered a soothing spell. Within seconds, I could feel the effects of my spell, and the tree stopped crying.

"You are okay," I whispered to the tree. "Once we get you fixed, I will do a healing spell so you will be good as new. I just need you to relax."

Over the last few months, I had been perfecting my healing

spells on plants and animals. It was a gift given to me from Black Forest King. Harnessing his power, I closed my eyes and pictured the damaged roots from the tree. Placing my hands atop the damaged roots, I wove the spell that would heal the splintered roots. Once they were whole again, I stood up, and using my magic, I levitated the tree and gently placed it back in the ground.

"Thank you, Shayla," Daisy said, wiping tears from her face. "I'm sure the angst I feel from the trees and flowers as a woodland fairy doesn't even compare to what you feel as a descendent from Black Forest King." She gave me a quick hug. "But even I could feel the agony of the oak tree."

"He's good as new now," I said, brushing the last of the tears from her cheek.

"Thanks to you, Princess," Needles said softly from my shoulder. *"You did a great job."*

The moment was shattered by the sound of the ambulance pulling into the back of the sheriff's station. Before the vehicle even stopped, the ambulance's back doors flew open, and one of the werewolf shifter paramedics hit the ground running.

23

It was nearing three by the time the paramedics left and Doc was released. We ushered Doc back inside the station, hoping to get some information from him.

"I'm sorry I can't be of any real help," Doc said. "I always park by that tree, so it wouldn't be hard for someone to find me there."

Grant looked up from the notebook he was writing in. "What time did you say you arrived at your lab?"

"Maybe around twelve-thirty," Doc said.

"More like one," Alex said. "Shayla and I left around one to go to her mom's for a late lunch and to see how Serenity's house fared in the daylight. Your vehicle wasn't here when we left the station."

Doc nodded. "That could be. So I arrived around one and left around two?"

Alex nodded. "I'd agree with that."

"And you didn't see anyone by your vehicle either time?" Grant asked.

Doc shook his head. "No. I'm sorry. But I also wasn't *looking* for anyone, either. I was focused on hearing what Finn might say about the bullet they took out of me last night, and I wanted to go over my notes again regarding Greta's murder. See if I missed anything."

"You're looking for someone advanced in magic," Opal said from her desk by the front door. "Not only did the person do a summoning spell, but they also cloaked themselves from another witch tracking them."

I nodded. "I've thought about that."

"So what's that leave?" Alex asked. "Witch?"

"And possibly fairy," I said.

Grant sighed. "Bernard Craft is a witch, and Seamus Oakleaf is a fairy. So we haven't gained much ground."

The front door burst open, and Serena bolted inside.

"I just heard what happened. Is Doc all right?"

"I'm fine," Doc said. "You didn't need to run all the way down here."

Serena waved her hand in the air dismissively. "It's only two blocks. Plus, I needed to tell someone what I saw."

Every head in the room jerked to Serena.

"What?" I demanded as I stood. "Did you see someone or something suspicious?"

"Maybe." Serena walked farther into the room and stopped near our desks. "I was in our back alley taking out the trash, when I heard someone running down the alleyway. I didn't think much about it. I had no idea what had happened to Doc yet. Anyway, when I turned to see who it was, all I saw was the back of the person. They had on a long black leather jacket that billowed out behind them as they—I wouldn't say they were running. It was more like speed walking. Like they didn't want to draw attention to themselves, but they needed to get somewhere fast."

"A long black leather jacket?" Alex mused. "Huh. I wonder if it was a coat and not a dress our witnesses saw?"

Grant nodded. "I bet it would be easy to mistake."

"Serena, did you get the impression the person was male or female?" I asked. "Did you get an idea or feel?"

Serena furrowed her brows. "I want to say male. I don't know why, but I do."

Grant stood and walked over to Serena, enveloping her in a hug. "This could really help us break the case." He leaned down and gave her a kiss. "You, dear wife, are a woman of many talents."

"Just trying to help. Well, I better get back to the bakery. We'd just closed and were sweeping up when all of this happened."

"Thank you for running down here and telling us," Alex said.

After Serena left, we went back to questioning Doc, hoping to get just a little more information from him. I was about to give up hope on discovering anything more when Opal's desk phone rang.

"You're kidding!" Opal stood and hung up the phone. "Dispatch just got a call about Christine Mossman. Her date came to pick her up and found her dead inside the house."

❧ 24 ❧

Alex and Grant both swore and jumped up from their chairs. Doc groaned and lowered his head into his hands.

"Poor Christine," Doc said. "Do you think she was murdered because of her friendship with Marta?"

"Don't think like that," I said. "It'll tear you up, which is exactly what the killer is hoping for."

"Do you think you can do this, Doc?" Alex asked. "If you can't, I'm sure I can ask a medical doctor at the hospital to come do the pronouncement and subsequent autopsy."

Doc stood and shook his head. "No. I got this. Not only is it my job, but I want to do everything I can to help you catch this heartless killer."

"Then let's go," Alex said.

Grant and Doc rode together in Grant's vehicle, while Alex, Needles, and I piled into Alex's Blazer.

"Once again," I said as I buckled the seatbelt, "it was a sleight-of-hand. Our killer gave us a distraction with Doc and having the tree fall on him and subsequent aftermath, while he went to Christine's house and killed her."

Grant, Finn, Doc, and the ambulance were already there by the time Alex parked in front of Christine's house.

"I'll stay here and keep watch," Needles said.

Alex and I hurried inside and grabbed a pair of booties from Finn.

"I just got here," she said. "I'm going to process the scene right now."

"Where's the guy who called it in?" Alex demanded.

"Paramedics are with him on the side of the house," Finn said.

Alex and I walked outside and waited until the same paramedic who'd treated Doc today finished giving the man oxygen. Nodding to us, the werewolf shifter stepped back and headed toward the ambulance.

"Can you tell us your name," Alex said, "and how it was you found the body?"

The man nodded. "Carson Nightsky. Vampire. I originally had a date with Christine for Valentine's Day, but then—" He cleared his throat. "Well, as you know, she was arrested and spent the night in jail. Then this morning, she called to say it was all a mistake, and would I like to go out for a picnic around four this afternoon." Carson smiled. "I figured why not? I own an online business, so my hours are flexible. I arrived at four, but Christine didn't answer. I called her cell phone and could hear it ringing right inside the door. Like she was standing right behind the door but not answering. I was a little put out, so I pounded again, then looked in the side window…" He trailed off. "That's when I saw her. I used my supernatural vampire strength and broke down the door." He shrugged and looked sheepish. "Sorry. But I wasn't thinking.

Anyway, I broke down the door, saw her on the floor, and called for help."

"You didn't notice anyone around when you arrived?" I asked.

Carson shook his head. "No."

"I'm sorry you had to experience this," Alex said. "Thanks for talking with us. If we have any more questions, we'll be in contact."

Carson nodded. "I'm sorry for what happened to her. She was a bright light. Loud and funny and full of life."

After he left, Alex and I headed back inside the house.

Doc stood from his kneeling position next to Christine's body and motioned us over. "Just like with Greta. Killer sliced her throat, then penned a note to her chest with a knife."

I waited until they removed the knife and bagged it for evidence before levitating the letter so we could all see it.

"I deserved to die. I was a betrayer of true friendship."

We all looked at each other, not saying anything. I figured they were like me—they didn't want to say the words aloud.

"So I was right," Doc finally said. "Christine was killed because of her friendship with Marta."

Alex motioned for Grant and me to follow him down a hallway.

"I want to try and catch our killer off guard," Alex said. "Grant, I'm going to call Deputy Sparks in early tonight. I want you two to go out to Bernard Craft's house and question him. Find out where he was this afternoon, search his house and get me the gun, the long coat, anything you can to prove he's the killer." Alex turned to me. "We're going to do the same for Seamus Oakleaf."

"Want me to get two warrants from Judge Lonewolf?" Grant asked.

Alex nodded. "Yes. Let him know we have sufficient probable cause for both men. He won't balk on this."

We walked back down the hallway toward Christine's body. The paramedics were helping Doc put her body on the stretcher.

"You guys finish up here," Grant said. "The courthouse is closed, so I'll have to go find Judge Lonewolf. Hopefully, he'll just be home, and I won't have to track him down." Grant looked outside. Dusk had already settled. "It's a full moon tonight. I doubt it'll be that easy."

"You know if he runs with a pack or alone?" Alex asked.

"Pack, ironically enough," Grant said. "And I know the pack, so I'll check there first."

"I'll take Doc and Christine back with me in the forensic van," Finn said. "That is, if you and Shayla can stay here and finish up?"

Alex nodded. "We can do that. Grant, text me the minute you have the warrants, and we'll meet up with you to get ours for Seamus Oakleaf."

25

"I don't think Seamus is home," I said.

We'd been banging on Seamus' front door for the past two minutes, but to no avail.

"He told us he's a loner and stays home," Alex said. "So where is he?"

I looked over at the dark forest surrounding his house. "Could be he's performing rituals tonight. Fairies and witches have certain ceremonies they perform on full-moon nights. Maybe he's in his woods."

Alex tried the door. It was locked.

"We have a warrant," Alex said. "We're going inside."

"Want me to zap the…"

My voice trailed off as Alex took a step backward, then kicked in the door with his foot.

"Or we can do it that way," I murmured.

"If Needles was here," Alex said as he took a step inside the darkened house, "he'd have praised my display of muscle."

I laughed and stepped inside Seamus' house as well. Needles

had only put up a small fight when I told him he needed to be with Zoie tonight as she drove to GiGi's house instead of with me. Reminding him there was still a killer on the loose kicked in his protection drive. No way would he let Zoie put herself in harm's way.

"Let me get us some light." I whispered a light orb spell so we could see inside the small cabin. "That's better."

"You check around here," Alex said, "and I'll check the rooms down the hallway."

The cabin was an open-concept, so the living room and kitchen made up the bulk of the area. I hurried to the kitchen and started pulling open drawers, hoping to find the gun. After opening every drawer and cabinet…I came up empty. I was searching through the closet by the front door when Alex walked into the room from down the hall.

"Nothing." He scanned the room. "I searched between the mattresses, under the nightstand, everywhere I could think to find the gun."

"Same here," I said. "I searched everywhere and didn't find the gun or his coat."

"I thought for sure we were on the right track."

"Now what?" I asked.

Alex's phone rang. "Hey, Grant. Anything?" He frowned. "Really? Same here. No, no. That's fine. See you in the morning."

"Well?" I asked when Alex disconnected.

"Grant and Sparks came up empty-handed as well. Bernard wasn't home, but they were still able to get inside."

I snorted. "Bernard probably figured there was no reason to ward his house. Only someone truly insane would break in to his house with the Lenas inside."

Alex nodded. "Agreed. Grant said the calendar in the

kitchen showed Bernard would be at a coven meeting starting at six. So they just missed him. He said the Lenas went about their business as if Grant and Sparks weren't even there. So they searched the house and came up empty-handed. They drove separately, so Grant is going home to run with Dash Stryker, and Sparks is on his way to patrol the south side of the island."

"What's our next move?" I asked.

"Let's go back to the station and see how Doc is coming along." We stepped outside, and Alex did his best to shut the broken door behind him. "If I know Doc, he's already started on the autopsy."

I hopped up inside the Blazer. "Poor Doc. In a matter of days, he's had two people in his life murdered, and he's having to deal with the ten-year anniversary of his wife's death."

I didn't say much on our ride back to town. I was too deep in thought about what we knew so far. Between our two major suspects, Bernard Craft and Seamus Oakleaf, I couldn't decide who had the most motive to hurt Doc. If I had to guess, I'd say Bernard. Seamus had lost his sister, Marta…but Bernard had lost his wife. I couldn't help but think the scales had to tip more in Bernard's favor for wanting Doc dead.

"You're lost in thought," Alex said as he parked in front of the sheriff's station. "Everything okay?"

I twisted the ring on my finger. "I've been thinking. Of our two suspects, who *really* lost the most that night ten years ago? I mean, Seamus lost Marta, his sister."

"But Bernard lost his wife of many years," Alex finished softly as his eyes zeroed in on my ring.

"Exactly."

We exited the Blazer, and Alex was about to unlock the front door when my phone rang.

"It's Jordan Owlman." I put him on speakerphone. "Hey, Jordan. What's up?"

"Have you heard from Finn?" he asked.

I frowned. "Finn? No. Why?"

"Because she sent me a text about fifty minutes ago saying she had to drop Doc off at the station, and then she'd drop by my house." He was talking so fast, his words were tripping over themselves. "I wouldn't be so worried if she'd pick up her phone, but she's not. I've called like thirty times, but it just goes to her voicemail. I don't know what to do. I'm worried."

Alex unlocked the front door, then pulled out his gun.

"Jordan, we're at the station now," I said. "We'll check and see if Finn is here, then call you back, okay?"

"Yeah, okay. I'm probably worrying for nothing."

I disconnected. "I doubt it."

Alex put his finger to his lips, opened the door, then quickly stepped inside, his gun drawn. I preferred using my magic. Stepping immediately behind him, I felt my magic humming through my body and sent the power to my fingertips.

I would be ready for anything.

The small foyer was empty, and the door to the right leading to the sheriff's office was dark inside. However, the stairs and basement were lit up nice and bright.

Taking the stairs side-by-side, Alex and I stopped at the bottom. A figure was lying in the middle of the hallway…unmoving.

"Finn!" I hissed, taking a step forward.

"Careful. We don't know who else is down here."

Knowing he was right, I forced myself to calm down and take in everything around me. Had Needles been here, I'd have sent him ahead to squeeze under Doc's door to see what was going on. But Needles wasn't here. Alex and I would be the ones to take down the killer that lurked somewhere inside the building.

By the time Alex and I finally reached Finn, my nerves were on fire. I needed to release the magical pent-up energy soon or I might explode.

Bending down, I rolled Finn over while Alex covered me. She moaned and opened her eyes. Before she could speak, I put my finger to my lips.

"Who else is here?" I whispered.

Before Finn could reply, a voice hollered from inside Doc's laboratory. "I know you and Alex have arrived, Shayla. Leave the girl outside where she is, and let's get this next part over with, shall we? Oh, and tell the gargoyle to put away his gun, or I'll kill Doc the minute you both step inside this room."

I looked up and met Alex's eyes.

In his human form, Alex didn't have access to his supernatural strength or his stone exterior—making him vulnerable to gunshots.

Alex holstered his gun, then pushed open Doc's door.

"Stay here," I whispered to Finn. "We'll get you untied once we finish this monster off."

The killer chuckled from inside Doc's office. "We will see about that, Witch."

26

I pushed Doc's door open wider and stepped inside next to Alex. The room was bright, so my eyes immediately went to Doc—tied up in a chair and slumped over.

Seamus Oakleaf stood behind Doc, holding a gun to Doc's head.

"He's alive," Seamus said. "But not for long. He's got enough drugs inside him to kill a—well, a dragon." Seamus laughed. "Have you figured it out yet?"

"Figured what out?" I asked. "You obviously killed Greta Twinkle and Christine Mossman. You aren't that complex. You did it for stupid, selfish reasons. And now you will pay for that with your life." I shrugged. "Either we kill you here or take you to PADA where they strip you of your powers and you spend the rest of your miserable life behind bars. I'm not picky. Either one works for me."

Seamus' face turned red. "It's more than that! I *deserve* retribution! I deserve to be compensated for what I lost!"

I snorted. "You lost your sister to an accident. She had an aneurysm and died. It sucks, but sometimes that's life."

"I've figured it out," Alex said beside me.

"Finally!" Seamus shouted. "Someone with brains."

"Hey!" I was pissed at the comment…but also confused. I was usually pretty quick on figuring things out—it's why I was one of the best agents PADA had before I retired. What had Alex figured out that I hadn't?

"You not only lost your sister," Alex said, "but you lost the woman you loved."

I frowned…then gasped as the piece to our unanswered question fell into place. "*You* were the man Lena Craft was having an affair with?"

"Yes! And in the blink of an eye, I lost both my sister and the only woman I've ever loved. All because the good doctor couldn't be bothered to concern himself with my sister's ailment!"

"But you live east of town," I said. "Lena wasn't coming from that direction."

"I only moved there after Lena and Marta died."

If I didn't have magic built up in my hands, I'd have smacked myself in the forehead. Of course! Hadn't Doc told us Seamus moved after Marta died to get away from everyone? Only it wasn't just Marta he lost…he also lost Lena.

"So you've been planning this for ten years?" I asked. "That's diabolical."

Seamus lifted the gun to the top of Doc's head. "I've been dreaming of ways to torment and kill this man since he carelessly ripped the women I loved from me. And I'm going to keep on doing it. Tonight, you both will die, as will the little fairy in the hallway. Let him try to live peaceably with that much blood on his hands."

Doc lifted his head. "Accccideeeent."

Fear shot through me. Doc's slurred speech, and the way his eyes rolled in his head told me he was seriously injured. His skin was clammy and pale. If he didn't get immediate help, he would die. In his drugged state, he couldn't shift, which meant he couldn't rid the effects from his body.

"So Greta Twinkle was a killing of convenience," I said. "What about Christine Mossman?"

"Christine came to visit me about a year after Marta and Lena had died. Told me how lonely she was without Marta, and then she went too far. Told me she even tried to get Doc to date her so she could have a little piece of Marta back. Like that somehow made it okay?" Spittle flew from his mouth. "And for that betrayal, I knew she had to pay. So I bided my time and waited until the ten-year anniversary. I sneaked into Christine's house when she was gone, stole a knife and hairs from one of her hairbrushes, and it was that simple. I set her up to take the fall…only you two wouldn't take the bait." He shrugged. "Not that it mattered. Because in the end, she had to die, and now I'm going to kill you two next."

"That's not going to happen," Alex said.

Alex shifted into his gargoyle form, and Seamus lifted the gun to shoot Alex. I raised my hands in the air and sent the stream of magic I'd been building straight at Seamus. The magic hit him in the chest, sending him flying backward. Unfortunately, the gun went off…hitting Alex in the face!

"You okay?" I screamed as I sent another wave of magic to Seamus, this time sending him rolling across the floor. When he hit the far wall, he stopped moving.

He was out cold.

"Yeah," Alex snarled, his voice deep and gruff. "Might leave a scar, though."

I let out a bark of laughter, lifted my binder from my belt, and threw it at Seamus. The binder activated, ensnarling Seamus in the invisible barrier. There was no way he could escape or use his magic.

"I'll fly Doc to your dad," Alex growled. "If anyone can help him, it's Black Forest King."

Alex reached for Doc.

Doc—obviously not understanding what was going on in his drugged state—panicked, let out a beastly roar, and somehow shifted.

Fire shot from Doc's mouth as his dragon broke free of the rope holding him captive. Alex and I instinctively ducked so we wouldn't get burned. Stumbling, Doc's dragon form turned around, his tail hitting Alex and sending him and the computer equipment careening across the room.

"Doc!" I screamed. "It's okay. Alex and I are trying to help. You have to calm down and shift back to human!"

But Doc was too far gone.

Sending out another blast of fire, he staggered toward the door. If he got to the hallway, he might accidentally crush Finn.

"I can't lift him now," Alex growled as he staggered to his feet. "Even in my gargoyle form, he's too big."

"I have an idea." Knowing I might hurt Doc more than help him, I closed my eyes and whispered a levitation spell. Doc immediately rose two feet in the air, thrashing and kicking. "I can't hold him long." My body shook from the effort of holding him in the air. "I need to get him outside."

Alex pushed open Doc's door, bent down and carefully lifted Finn in his arms, then ran to the back door and kicked it open using his supernatural power.

Doc was so large, his dragon body knocked enormous holes

in the hallway walls as I levitated him up the stairs and out the back door.

Setting him on the ground, I whispered a soothing spell to calm him down, then closed my eyes and focused on my next move. There was only one person who could help us now.

Randor.

Randor wasn't a dragon shifter. He was an actual dragon who was thousands of years old. He often roamed the night sky on the north side of the island. If I could focus enough, I might be able to communicate with him through my link that allowed me to talk to other plants and animals.

"Randor! Can you hear me? It's Shayla Loci. I need your help! Please! Can you hear me?"

It only took a few seconds before I had my answer.

"I can hear you, Daughter of Black Forest King. What can I do to help?"

"I'm at the sheriff's station. Doc, one of your descendants, has been hurt. He needs your help. And the help of Black Forest King. I know you don't usually come into town, but do you think you can help me? Please!"

"Worry not, Shayla Loci. I shall come now."

I opened my eyes. "Randor is on his way. We need to step back and give him plenty of room."

Alex, who'd shifted back to human, pulled Finn close and helped her walk over to the forensic van. Opening the door, he set her down and tended to the gash on her forehead. I was about to do a healing spell to help out, when the air changed and Randor streaked across the sky, then dropped and landed in the parking lot. Folding his wings, he lumbered across the asphalt and stood next to me.

Doc was a gigantic dragon…but standing next to Randor, he now looked like a baby kitten.

"He's been drugged," I said. *"I'm afraid if he doesn't get help soon, he may die."*

"He cannot shift back to human?"

"No! He's disoriented. I've given him a soothing spell to help, but I can't levitate him to see Dad. He's too big."

Randor nodded, causing a puff of smoke to shoot out of his nostrils. *"I shall carry him to see Black Forest King, Shayla Loci. You must stand back. I do not want my wings to hit you."*

"Thank you, Randor."

I ran over to Alex and Finn as Randor opened his mouth and clamped down around the middle of Doc's dragon form. I winced, hoping Doc couldn't feel it, then watched in amazement as Randor's wings expanded and lifted them both in the air.

"You okay?" I asked Finn.

She nodded, then groaned. "Seamus hit me over the head with the butt of his gun."

"You got a pretty good gash," Alex said.

"So do you." I reached up and wiped the blood off his cheek.

"My face isn't near as hard as my body when I shift."

I nodded. "You're right. You'll probably have a scar."

"We're a mess," Finn said, "but at least we're all alive."

Alex took out his phone. "I'll call PADA so they can send someone out to pick up Seamus, and then I'll fly you out to see your dad and make sure Doc is okay."

27

Dad was able to save Doc once Randor had gotten Doc to Black Forest. Not that I was worried…much. Dad had communicated to Needles he needed help, and since Needles, Zoie, and Mom were at GiGi's, they all ended up at Black Forest helping Doc recover.

Finn had taken one of my soothing spells while Alex and I drove her to Jordan's house. Deputy Sparks had been called in and he stayed with Seamus until someone from PADA could arrive.

By the time Alex flew me to Black Forest to check on Doc, it was almost ten o'clock. Doc was still groggy, but could confirm what Finn had told us. Seamus had ambushed them at the station when Doc and Finn had unloaded Christine's body. Seamus had held the gun on Finn and had forced her to inject Doc with the drugs. Doc said he was too scared to shift in case Seamus shot Finn. Once the drugs took effect, Seamus hit Finn over the head and tied her and Doc up.

Then he waited until Alex and I showed up.

Just as we were all about to leave and go home for the night, Mom announced she wanted to have a family get-together Friday night in Black Forest.

I was a little surprised.

Dad was particular about who he allowed inside his sanctuary, so it was a big deal to have not only Mom, GiGi, Alex, Zoie, and me inside the forest all at once, but Serena, Grant, and Aunt Starla were also invited to the get-together.

* * *

"I'm sure you're all wondering why I asked for this meeting?" Mom stood and faced Dad's trunk. "Truth is, Black Forest King and I wanted you all here."

I gasped and glared at Needles.

"I told you I have no idea what this is about, Princess."

"And he is right." Dad's voice echoed in all our heads. *"Your mother and GiGi have only let me in on what is going on."*

"What's this about, Mom?" I demanded. "Are you guys okay?"

"Everything is fine," Mom soothed.

GiGi stood as well and wrapped an arm around Mom's waist. "Shayla, have you and Alex given any thought to where you'll live once you're married?"

"Not really," I said.

"At the castle," Zoie piped up. "I want that kitchen in the marriage."

Everyone laughed at Zoie's response.

"I can't say I blame her," Serena said.

"GiGi and I have been talking," Mom said, "and I'm hoping you will do something for me, Shayla."

"Of course," I said. "Anything."

Mom smiled. "I was hoping you might give me a section of land between the castle and Black Forest. I'd like to build a small cottage and live back there, where I was meant to live."

Tears filled my eyes. Mom wanted to live next to Dad? I hadn't seen that coming. "Of course. This land is yours, Mom. Not mine. Dad built the castle for you. You can have the castle if you'd like."

Mom shook her head. "No. I don't need anything that large. It was nice when you, Serena, Aunt Starla, and I all lived there, but now the castle is ready to make new memories. Memories with you, Alex, and Zoie."

Alex brushed a thumb across my cheek, wiping away a tear that had fallen from my eye.

"You can have whatever land you want," I said.

"Thank you, Daughter of my Heart," Dad said. *"You have always been a blessing to your mother and me."*

"Which brings us to our next announcement," GiGi said.

Aunt Starla groaned. "I'm not sure I can take much more."

GiGi grinned. "You may be quite shocked at this, Starla." GiGi took a deep breath. "I think it's time I moved into town. It's becoming harder and harder for me to drive my Vespa around the island. My old bones are beginning to feel it."

"You don't even have a license," Alex grumbled.

Again, everyone laughed.

GiGi reached down and lifted my cousin, Serena, to her feet. "Serena, I'd like to give you and Grant my cottage. I know you two have been looking for a place out of town, and I think it's only fair you have my house."

Serena let out a little scream and threw her arms around GiGi. "Are you sure?"

GiGi nodded. "I'm sure." She untangled herself from Serena. "Would that be okay with you, Grant?"

Grant grinned, stood up, and hugged GiGi. “Knowing how much it would please Serena is all that matters to me. We’ve been looking and can’t find anything. So if you’re sure, I think it’s a great idea.”

“Where will you live, GiGi?” Zoie asked. “In Grant and Serena’s house?” Her eyes widened. “Or you could have our house when we move into the castle.”

GiGi shook her head. “No. I’m going to move into Serenity’s house. It’s a good location in town, and I’ll be happy there.”

“It’s also closer to Byron Sealy,” I joked.

GiGi scowled at me…but I just grinned.

“You know what that means?” Zoie asked me.

“What?” I mused.

“You and Serena will be neighbors.”

I grinned and hugged my cousin. “Just like when we were young.”

“This is a night for celebration,” Dad said. *“For new beginnings and new adventures.”*

* * *

After everyone had left Black Forest and gone home, I stayed behind to talk with Dad. It was just me and Needles, leaning lazily against Dad’s trunk, listening to the forest sounds around us.

“What is on your mind, Daughter of my Heart? Are you not happy with the decisions made here tonight?”

I sat up straighter. “That’s not it at all. I’m stoked about all the changes coming down the pike.” I settled back against his trunk. “I wanted to talk about something I saw on the southeast side of the island.”

“What have you found?” Dad asked.

"I saw two drag marks along the sand that went from the water to the forest. Well, actually, I can't tell if the tracks go from the water to the forest or from the forest to the water."

"What is your concern?"

I frowned. "I don't know exactly. I've never seen drag marks like them. They weren't made from an animal or a human, I don't think."

"Did you ask the animals?" Dad asked.

"No. I haven't had time yet. Alex and I were busy catching Seamus, but now that that's taken care of, I think I need to go back down to the water's edge on the southeast side and see what's going on."

"I think that would be best," Dad said. *"We wouldn't want something unknown entering Enchanted Island."*

* * *

Are you ready for the next book in the series, Deadly Vines? Then click here: My Book

* * *

Love the idea of a Valkyrie witch teaming up with a Fallen Angel to solve crimes? Then the paranormal cozy series, A Kara Hilder Mystery, should be right up your alley! This crime-solving duo not only works for their supernatural town of Mystic Cove, but they also work for the Paranormal Apprehension and Detention Agency—which means they travel a lot to take down bad guys. Find out what happens when a Valkyrie with magical abilities teams up with a Fallen Angel in Book 1, Sounds of Murder My Book

. . .

Do you love the idea of a time-traveling, cold-case solving witch? Then Lexi and her side-kick detective familiar, Rex the Rat, are just what you're looking for! Check out their first stop to 1988 in Time After Time My Book

Have you read the hilarious adventures of Ryli Sinclair and Aunt Shirley? Book 1 is Picture Perfect Murder! My Book

Love the idea of a bookstore/bar set in the picturesque wine country of Sonoma County? Then join Jaycee, Jax, Gramps, Tillie, and the whole gang as they solve murders while slinging suds and chasing bad guys in this hilarious series. My Book

How about a seaside mystery? My stepdaughter and I write a mystery where high school seniors pair up with their grandma and great-aunt! Book one, Seaside & Homicide: My Book

Or maybe you're in the mood for a romantic comedy…heavy on comedy and light on sweet romance? Then the Trinity Falls series is for you! My Book

. . .

Looking for a paranormal cozy series about a midlife witch looking to make a new start with a new career? Then A Witch in the Woods is the book series for you! A game warden witch, a talking/flying porcupine, and a gargoyle sheriff! My Book

ABOUT THE AUTHOR

Jenna writes in the genres of cozy/paranormal cozy/ romantic comedy. Her humorous characters and stories revolve around over-the-top family members, creative murders, and there's always a positive element of the military in her stories. Jenna currently lives in Missouri with her fiancé, step-daughter, Nova Scotia duck tolling retriever dog, Brownie, and her tuxedo-cat, Whiskey. She is a former court reporter turned educator turned full-time writer. She has a Master's degree in Special Education, and an Education Specialist degree in Curriculum and Instruction. She also spent twelve years in full-time ministry.

When she's not writing, Jenna likes to attend beer and wine tastings, go antiquing, visit craft festivals, and spend time with her family and friends. Check out her website at http://www.jennastjames.com/. Don't forget to sign up for the newsletter so you can keep up with the latest releases! You can also friend request her on Facebook at jennastjamesauthor/ or catch her on Instagram at authorjennastjames.

Made in United States
North Haven, CT
31 December 2024

63789168R00085